AUNT PEDRINA

AUNT PEDRINA

(Growing Up in Brazil)

Noel Gordo

With Special Assistance from Hobbs Horak

VANTAGE PRESS
New York

This is a work of fiction. Any similarity between the names and characters in this book and any real persons, living or dead, is purely coincidental.

Cover design by Susan Thomas

FIRST EDITION

Published by Vantage Press, Inc.
419 Park Ave. South, New York, NY 10016

Manufactured in the United States of America
ISBN: 978-0-533-15469-2

Library of Congress Catalog Card No.: 2006901494

0 9 8 7 6 5 4 3 2 1

Acknowledgments

Barbara Esstman
for her professional editing and friendship

Dr. Regina Igel
for her constructive and insightful criticism

Julie Carson
for her love, consideration, and unlimited encouragement

Dr. Francisco Antonio Torres
a great friend who provided me with invaluable guidance

Author's Note

Sixteen exceptional and quite different women inspired me to write this book, which is fiction, not anyone's biography. It was carefully crafted to give the reader the impression that every opinion and suggestion was the action of a single woman; the symbol I developed to represent each one of them, Aunt Pedrina.

AUNT PEDRINA

One
A Beautiful Spring Day

A pleasant breeze of fresh air, carrying the gentle scent of new life, was wafting through the trees and shrubs. A potpourri of essence from the many different flowers impregnated the air. The flower bed of African daisies, an array of colors, was solidly covered with flowers. Daisies are hardy plants; they bloom longer than most other plants. All the other flowers were beautiful, but the daisies, with their white petals and bright yellow center, looked like they were smiling, like they were pleased to be there. They were Aunt Pedrina's favorite flower. All around, there was a harmonious sound of insects. They hummed and buzzed, inebriated with the dizzying variety of color and perfume, but mostly, animated by the intensity of light.

The sun was bright, but not hot. Birds were diving in all directions, interlacing, creating an exotic choreography against the blue sky. They probably were also excited with the beauty of the day. And, it was on this beautiful day that Aunt Pedrina died. She would never have departed on an ugly, rainy, winter day.

I was in my late teens. I had never experienced losing someone to whom I was very close. From the hospital, her body was taken to a special room in the church reserved for the viewing, the same church where she was baptized and had been married a long time ago. Aunt Dolores and cousin

Julia had cut the African daisies from the yard and placed them over her body in the casket. Carefully, they had arranged the flowers, forming a blanket. She looked very old, sleeping among her favorite flowers. I knew she was close to ninety.

When I used to visit her, I spent many hours in her little studio talking, mostly about school. I remember telling her stories about my chemistry class, all the strange tubes and mixtures we used to work with to prepare unusual concoctions of curious liquids, and carefully pouring them together inside one of the glass tubes. It was exciting to watch the liquid in the tube go up in a smoke of varying colors or maybe change to a bright orange. For the teacher, that was chemistry, but for me it was magic. Aunt Pedrina used to laugh heartily at my excitement with chemistry. No other adult was ever genuinely interested in my school adventures, but she enjoyed hearing whatever I had to say. I never thought about her as an old person. Now, lying in the casket, she had a calm expression, like she was just taking a nap.

I sat down in a corner of the room; I wanted to be left alone. It was hard for me to accept that she was gone forever. The idea that I would never again be able to talk with her was devastating. Why do people have to die? It was a difficult concept for a young person to fully understand.

The room, in dimmed light, was very quiet. The casket was placed on a tall platform completely covered with purple fabric. At each of the four corners of the platform, a tall candleholder made of dark, carved wood made the casket look solemn and impressive. Except for the chairs along the walls and some wood pedestals with flowers arranged about them, there was not much furniture. The windows were dressed with the same heavy, burgundy fabric that covered the platform. Everyone was whispering, creating a mantra, bouncing off the stone walls. Most of the aggrieved were old people, dressed in dark clothes. The air was heavy with the perfume of flowers mixed with the strong smell of burning candle wax. In that moment of solitude and pain I began to think about my own mortality. Is death the end of everything or the beginning of a new phase? Do we really have an immortal soul? If we do, where does it go after one dies?

Later, some of my cousins arrived, looking confused and awkward, like a bunch of lost and scared kids holding back tears. We knew we had lost a great friend.

You are probably thinking it is too morbid to start Aunt Pedrina's story on the day she passed away. But, please, don't judge me wrongly. My intention is to protect you. I don't want you to get to know her, learn about all the naughty and nice things she did, let you feel the compassion and love she always demonstrated to every human and animal, big and small, let you fall in love with her, and then, later, much later, let you go through the pain of losing her. I will never forget that perfect, beautiful, and very sad spring day.

Two
Getting to Know Her

Aunt Pedrina was born in the 1880s in Mirante, a small village southeast of Sao Paulo, Brazil. The village was located on a bluff overlooking a river, surrounded by mountains standing two miles distant. She was born and lived there all her life. Before it became a city, the owners of coffee farms in that region and the workers of those farms used to go to the bluff on Sundays for a picnic or just to sit there, enjoying the view and waiting for the sun to set. Everyone called that area Mirante, which in Portuguese means a place to look out. It is a city that was never planned, it just grew, like a wildflower. Gramma told me that her father, my great-grandfather, was among the first coffee farm owners to build a house on the bluff. Gradually they started to make Mirante their permanent home. It took some time for Mirante to be considered a city. They didn't have a mayor until they decided they needed a post office. In order to have a post office, they had to make the city official, and elect their first mayor.

A woman of strong spirit and an even stronger desire to live her life to the fullest, Aunt Pedrina had progressive opinions about many things, especially about our responsibility toward protecting and respecting the world around us. She lived way before her time; it was like she lived in the future. You would never hear her say how good it was before, but always how much better it could become. Her today was, in many instances, next year for many others. She believed it is our obligation to improve ourselves and was never uncomfortable about saying she was sorry, and when she did say it, we had no doubt she really meant it. But just a minute, don't get too comfortable: she could be intimidating sometimes. Her favorite questions were: "Why?" and "Why not?" My cousins and I always had to make clear our answers by explaining all the factors that had led to our understanding of the problem. Maybe it was because she was and forever continued to be a teacher. She always wanted to make sure we had learned something.

She had a special way to show affection. She disliked mushy stuff, so her best way to show her love was by helping us overcome the obstacles we encountered. She knew and accepted that we were not perfect, but she always made sure we understood we were not helpless, either. It was like she placed herself in our position, so she could fully understand our inability to comprehend the complexity of a situation because of our young age.

In situations where she could not help us successfully overcome the problem, she would help us to understand that we didn't have all the necessary tools, yet. She would guide us to accept the temporary setback and incorporate it into our learning reality in preparation for the future. Most of the time she made us feel comfortable with ourselves by accepting completely what we were and being proud of it. I don't know any more convincing kind of love than that. Anyone can love a hero, but it takes a special person to love and understand someone who is losing a battle.

If one of us appeared to be unhappy, she would ask, "Why the long face?" She wanted to know what was causing the problem. After our explanation, she would just say, "O.K. It doesn't sound very good, but what have you planned to do about it? How do you propose to change this unpleasant situation into an acceptable one? Let's see if we can find a solution." I recall one occasion when I was upset because a classmate had stolen one of my books. I didn't know how to handle the situation or what would be the best thing I could do to get my book back.

"Can you prove that the book was your book?" she asked.

"Yes," I said, "I bought the book in the bookstore at the school. I still have the receipt. I also signed my name on the last page, like I do with all my books."

"Good! I don't think you have a problem. You tell the boy, very politely, that you have ways to prove he took your book. Tell him if he returns the book voluntarily, you will forget the incident. However, if he refuses to do so, you will go to the principal and will report the problem."

"Why do I have to be polite?" I asked, puzzled. "He's a bad person."

With a generous smile, she said, "I know, but you are not. On many occasions, when we act calm and polite, we become more believable and appear to be much more dangerous." She was right. The boy became extremely uncomfortable and I believe a little scared. He gave me the book back and walked away without saying anything.

She refused to be a victim in any circumstance and would not allow us to become one, either. Every time someone did or tried to do something that offended or hurt one of us, she would tell us that nothing and no one has the right or the power to dominate us or control our emotions and decisions. She would listen to everything we had to say very carefully, and tried hard to understand our point of view. She would never pass judgment on anything before she had a chance to learn all the facts, and always showed compassion and consideration to our way of thinking. In fact, we never had reason to doubt that she respected all of us. But we couldn't ever take her for granted or think she was a weak character. We could always count on her understanding and help, but we were unable to fool her.

According to Aunt Pedrina, the only alternative for right was wrong. If it was not right, it was definitely wrong. She had no problem in accepting that we may have had a legitimate reason to be wrong, but she made sure we knew that we should never try to deceive others or try to manipulate the situation and present it as right. Anytime one of us did something wrong, she never criticized in a negative way and totally avoided saying, "You're wrong." She would rather say, "Sorry, but you are not right." She would give us a chance to explain our misconception. Then, very patiently, she would help us establish the difference between right and wrong. And she always finished that particular lesson by saying the same thing, "Don't worry too much about it, growing up is sometimes a complicated process. One of these days you will be able to figure out all those things, all by yourself." Gramma would always say Aunt Pedrina was born a teacher; she loved to learn and teach new things.

In the early 1900s, women did not have many choices for a career. Grammar school teacher was one of the most acceptable jobs for a young woman, probably because if they were trained to be a grammar school teacher, they would acquire the necessary skills to become a good mother. She was graduated from the Normal School, what is now Teachers' College, and became a grammar school teacher. After graduation, she returned to her hometown and started her career. She had just started teaching at Saint Agnes, a private school for girls, when she married her childhood sweetheart, Uncle Luiz, who had become a young officer in the army. Everyone who knew them considered them a perfect couple, very much in love with each other.

They had grown up in Mirante, where they both had been born and lived with their respective families, who were plantation owners and were part of the community from the beginning. As the little town grew, so did the population. Many of the residents who worked as domestic servants came from the farms. There were people who had come from other places, who worked in different stores at the small shopping center, at one of the two banks, the post office, the only movie theater, or as public workers for the city office, and who kept Mirante the pride of its residents and founders. There were teachers and office workers at the only public school, which had classes from first to twelfth grade. There were also two private schools. It was a place where everyone knew everyone and knew everything about everybody.

Pedrina and Luiz had been good friends since they were small kids. They went to the same schools; she was two years behind Luiz. The only time they were separated for a long period of time was when he went to the Military Academy and she to Normal School. Both schools were out of town.

Gramma told me that when Aunt Pedrina was a little girl, everyone loved to ask her the same question again and again because of the cute way she always answered it.

"Pedrina, what are you going to do when you grow up?"

"I'm going to get married," she used to answer, quite sure of herself.

"And, whom are you going to marry?" was the traditional follow-up question.

"My husband, Luiz," she would answer, without hesitation and matter-of-factly. And she did just that.

Every Sunday they would go to church together, arm in arm, greeting everyone. She loved parading her young officer in his shining uniform.

Aunt Pedrina was Gramma's younger sister. Gramma told me Aunt Pedrina's wedding was a big social event in the little town. The whole population knew them well and almost everyone was invited.

"Everyone? The entire city?"

"Oh, no. When Pedrina got married, Mirante was still a small village. The whole population was nothing like it is today."

"So, everybody would fit inside the church?"

"Well, it was a small population, but not that small. People who received invitations had a place in the church. Those who weren't invited came anyway and stood in front of the church."

Pedrina and Maggie were very good friends since the time they were little girls. Maggie knew a dressmaker in the capital who had become well known for designing brides' gowns. They went together to have Pedrina's gown made by this famous dressmaker. The whole village knew the story about the dress and wanted to see it. So everyone was excited, waiting for the bride. Actually, waiting for the gown.

Aunt Pedrina kept a large photo of her wedding on a small, round table in the living room of her house. I always admired that photo. They looked thoroughly happy.

Before they got married, she quit her job as a teacher and stayed home preparing herself to be a wife and, eventually, mother. That was the way in those days. Uncle Luiz bought a newly remodeled colonial brick house that was located on the same street of Gramma's house. It was a well-built, two-story residence. The front entrance had a tall portico with white columns, finished with a small, white rail on the top. The windows had wooden louvered shutters, also painted white.

Together, they planted a beautiful front garden and oversaw the construction of a flagstone walk. Carefully, they selected several different flowers, which bloomed all year around. In the backyard, they planted a variety of fruit trees. They turned this house into a warm and comfortable home, where they were planning to live for a long time. Aunt Pedrina loved flowers and trees. She had a special affection for African daisies, so she reserved one side of the flower bed just for daisies.

They did not have any children. She didn't have a chance to be a wife for very long. Uncle Luiz died before their first wedding anniversary. He was killed in a terrible accident during an army maneuver. I never learned all the details about the accident. The family avoided talking about this unfortunate tragedy that undoubtedly changed Aunt Pedrina's life forever. Everyone refrained from making any comment in order not to cause more pain to Aunt Pedrina. Besides, it happened many years before I was born. Time has the tendency to fade the clarity of old images.

When I learned about Uncle Luiz's untimely death, I asked Gramma about the accident. She was quiet for a brief moment, like she was thinking, then she told me it was something she didn't like to remember. However, she told me that Aunt Pedrina was devastated by Uncle Luiz's death. She stayed secluded for a long time and wouldn't go anyplace, not even to the church. She didn't receive any visitors, either. The only one she would talk to was Father Giordano from her church; he had baptized her and also officiated at her wedding. He was like a member of the family. After all, he had been a presence in the important moments of her life.

Gramma told me the whole family had been fearfully concerned about her. Everyone was giving Olinda, her housekeeper, instructions to keep a constant, watchful eye. She was told to contact Gramma if she noticed anything unusual. The general opinion was that Aunt Pedrina would not survive Uncle Luiz's death.

Three
Oops!

One morning, without any indication why, Aunt Pedrina got up, got dressed, and told Olinda she was going to see her sister. Olinda followed her to the front gate and watched until she reached Gramma's house. She had not left home for several months, since Uncle Luiz's funeral.

When she arrived, Gramma was quite surprised, but very pleased to see her up and around.

"Oh, Pedrina! It is wonderful to see you, finally, out of your bedroom and getting around again."

"Oh, thanks," she responded somberly.

"How are you?" Gramma said, first taking Pedrina's hands and studying her face, and then embracing her warmly, "I missed seeing you and talking with you."

"I missed you too, Alice. I'm sorry for causing so much concern to the family. Unfortunately, I was in no condition to talk to anyone. I needed time alone to organize my thoughts and decide what to do with my life," she explained, her expression vague and distant.

Gramma put her arm around Aunt Pedrina's shoulder and they moved in the direction of the kitchen table, the favorite spot for all the important family talks. "I understand. You're going through a very difficult ordeal, but let's sit down and have a good cup of coffee." She was trying to avoid bringing sad memories to that special moment. "We just finished baking an orange cake. It's bright yellow and smells and tastes delicious. Would you like a slice with your coffee?"

"That's nice," Aunt Pedrina answered, "I need some time with you. I have something I want to tell you."

"Oh, good. Let's have coffee and talk, like we used to."

"Alice," Aunt Pedrina began and then paused, looking through the window with her eyes lost into nowhere. "I'm tired of my lethargy. The days become too long when we have nothing to do. I've been brooding, crying, and suffering long enough. I know that what happened to me was a tragedy that hurt me very much and I'll never forget. Sometimes I feel like I'm having a bad dream and I just have to wake up and everything is going to be in the right place, including Luiz. Other times I feel this enormous empty space in my chest that gradually becomes full of pain, an excruciating pain. I have to control myself not to scream, a loud and long scream. It's been so difficult. But I cannot spend the rest of my life being angry and secluded. I don't believe it's what Luiz would expect of me. I'm thinking about going back to teach."

"Pedrina! How wonderful," Gramma exclaimed happily, standing up and embracing her sister. "What a marvelous idea! You're a good teacher and you have always loved to teach. I'm sure St. Agnes will be thrilled to have you back."

Aunt Pedrina frowned and stiffened like someone had poked her with a needle. She looked at her sister with a poignant, penetrating stare and said, "No, Alice, I'm sorry, but I don't wish to go back to St. Agnes. In fact, I don't wish to go back to anywhere. I'm not a phoenix. It isn't my intention to rise and rebuild my life out of what was left from my tragedy. I want to build a new life, experience new challenges, do something meaningful for others rather than just for myself."

Gramma was puzzled; she had an expression as if she were lost in the woods. "I'm sorry, too, Pedrina, but I'm not sure if I understand what you're trying to say. What do you have in mind, exactly?"

Without paying too much attention to Gramma's reaction, she answered, almost mechanically, "I'm going to teach in the schoolhouse in Indian Creek."

"What?" Gramma almost shrieked. She got up and started to talk, much louder than her usual tone of voice, which was, according to herself, not permissible for a perfect lady. "Pedrina, you're not making any sense. Teaching at the schoolhouse in Indian Creek is absolutely impossible. The only way to get to Indian Creek is to go to the end of town, cross the little bridge, and then drive all the way back on the other side of the river. The road on the other side is in terrible condition. The only way is travel by horse or truck. You're not thinking of moving to Indian Creek, are you?"

"No, Alice, I'm not going to move to Indian Creek, and I'm well aware of the distance from here to the bridge as well as the bad condition of the road."

The Indian Creek schoolhouse was located in the south part of Mirante, in the Indian Creek Village. The village and its inhabitants were separated from the rest of town by the river. It was the poorest part of the town. The only access to the village was a small bridge on the west end of town. There were only small farms and poverty. No one from town wanted to go there and no one wanted anybody from there to come to town.

They built the bridge so far away for economic reasons. The river is much narrower at the end of town. So, they could build a small and inexpensive bridge out of everyone's sight. The bridge was necessary for the farmers from Indian Creek Village to bring their crops to town, allowing the residents to have fresh fruits and vegetables for a low price.

"Do you know, Alice, the schoolhouse is closed most of the time? No one wants to go teach there. The kids over there don't have anything. I want to give them a chance to get, at least, a basic education, to help them to have a better life." For a short time there was complete silence. Gramma continued to look at her sister in disbelief. She could not fully comprehend the meaning of that conversation. Finally, like she was awoken from a bad dream, she spoke.

"Pedrina, everything you are saying is true and thoughtful. I agree with almost everything. Your idea is a noble one, but I can't see how you're going to accomplish your goal. You must make a realistic evaluation of the situation. You have to accept things as they are."

Aunt Pedrina, giving in to a half smile and dreamy expression, spoke as if she were talking to herself, "If we had a bridge right here where we live, I could be there in fifteen minutes . . . fifteen minutes."

"Pedrina, wake up," Alice demanded. "You're dreaming. Give yourself more time. You're still going through a very difficult situation. You must regain your emotional and physical strength. It's natural that you wish to do something right now to help you overcome your grief; however, the city is not going to build a bridge over here so you can go teach in Indian Creek."

"I know that," Aunt Pedrina answered, matter-of-factly, "I also know that we must build our own bridges to get where we want to go. We are all alone when the time comes to cross over."

"Oh, now you're being philosophical. You're making me nervous," Gramma complained. She stood and turned quickly, and marched over to the stove to get more coffee. For the moment, she kept her back to Pedrina.

"No, Alice, I'm not being philosophical. I'm being practical. I'm going to buy a canoe and paddle myself to the other side of the river. It will take about fifteen minutes. And that will be my bridge." Aunt Pedrina smiled as if she had just discovered water in the desert.

Gramma spun around, furious, making an enormous effort to keep the conversation civil, but Aunt Pedrina's attitude was making it very difficult, almost impossible. "My goodness, Pedrina! I can't believe what I'm hearing. You are insane!" Now, Aunt Pedrina was the one who was losing composure and becoming irritated with her sister.

"Alice, I'm the one having trouble understanding your reaction. I can't see anything inconceivable with my plan. What's wrong with my idea?"

At that time, early 1900s, there were many things that nice girls didn't do, especially in that little town where Aunt Pedrina and Gramma were members of an upper class family. For Gramma it was inconceivable for a young woman in Aunt Pedrina's position to participate in any public sporting activities, much less paddling a canoe.

"What's wrong? The embarrassment, the ridicule, of the situation. What everyone will say about you paddling a canoe back and forth on the river. That is what's wrong. We have a name and a social position in this little town. Everyone knows you, our parents, grandparents, and me. Does the family's reputation mean anything to you?" At that point, the conversation was a little too loud. Yolanda, Gramma's housekeeper, was standing in the kitchen doorway, ready to interfere, if it became necessary.

"I have as much respect for the family and the family reputation as you do. But we are talking about my life, my dreams, and my desire to do something for others who are in more need than you, I, or the family, or our reputation. And that is what I'm going to do whether you like it or not."

"Pedrina, I will do everything in my power to stop you. You can't do that!"

"Why not? Give one good reason why I should not do it."

"Pedrina, for God's sake, be reasonable. It's not lady-like to go paddling a canoe. People will talk."

"I don't care what anyone thinks or says about me. Public opinion does not affect me. If they think I'm not a lady, it's fine with me. I'm not a LADY. I'm a teacher! Good day!" Aunt Pedrina was enraged. She left, banging the door behind her. They didn't speak to each other for some time.

Four

The Great Negotiator

Aunt Pedrina had decided that nothing would interfere with her project and was in the process of establishing a strategy to execute the plan. She recognized the need to engage a few other players in order to make the plan a complete success. Each one would have a specific function and would be recruited at the right time. She was also developing a strategy to involve the entire community in the project. Individuals and organizations would have a part to play. The first one on her list was Juca.

Juca was a renowned character in town, not just because of his unconventional and colorful personality, but most of all, for his ability as a gardener. He was a child of a farming family who had migrated from the northeast when he was a baby. Juca was a small fellow, about 5'7", slightly built, and easily recognized by the over-sized straw hat he always wore. The hat had become his trademark.

Everyone used him for garden work. He knew every possible plant by name and the best way to cultivate it. He was well-liked and respected, a good soul, always happy. When he wasn't working in somebody's garden, he was in the river, fishing or just paddling his canoe and enjoying the river he loved. He was not the brightest person, but with his goodness and ever-present smile, he would easily befriend all those he met, many of them for life.

Nobody would pay much attention to his fantastic stories about the river. He knew it so well, thanks to his canoe. Juca was the local authority about canoes. When it came to canoes, he sure knew all there was to be known.

Aunt Pedrina was aware of that. She liked listening to him talk about the river when he came to work in the yard. She often bought fish from him, whenever he caught a good one. The fish always came with a good story, which she would patiently let him tell. She was a good customer as well as a good listener. Juca always felt at ease around her.

One morning she asked Olinda to go look for Juca. Finding him was not difficult. The city was small and everyone knew him. Aunt Pedrina told Olinda to ask him to come by the house when he finished work. She had a few questions to ask him.

He was happy when he arrived, pleased to have someone interested in what he had to say, and Aunt Pedrina was extremely interested. They sat in the backyard under the shade of an old orange tree. She asked Olinda to bring lemonade with lots of ice because it was a warm summer afternoon. Sipping lemonade, they talked for a long time. When he left, she knew all about canoes and knew exactly the best one to buy.

They made arrangements for Juca to teach her how to paddle and handle a canoe. The next morning, very early, they met on the riverbank to start practicing in Juca's canoe, which was clean and polished especially for Dona Pedrina.

Her "Operation Canoe" was going better than she had anticipated. She was learning fast about how handle a canoe and was making progress paddling and maneuvering. So, the time was perfect for her to initiate the second phase of the project, which was the one she liked best, playing politics. She made an appointment and went to see Afonso Correia, the city's mayor. She knew him and his family well. She had grown up with his younger sister, who continued to be a good friend of hers. Aunt Pedrina and Correia had known each other for all their lives. He was like a big brother to her and she knew how to push the right buttons to inflate his ego and manipulate his decisions to her advantage.

She also knew that Correia was a busy man. Besides being the mayor, he was involved with many other businesses and was the owner of the largest coffee farm in the region. For this reason, she spoke directly to the purpose that had brought her to his office. In detail, she explained to him her plan to help the children of Indian Creek have access to basic education. His help was vital due to the deplorable condition of the schoolhouse, which was a public school, and the only school existent on the other side of the river. The building needed urgent repairs. Actually, it had to be rebuilt.

Of course, he told her that at that moment there was no budget available for the project. She knew he was going to say that; she was prepared. If he had said yes immediately, it wouldn't have been fun. She knew how to play the game and she was getting in position to start.

"Correia, you know as well as I do that a government budget is a very flexible organism. It is unbelievable how many miracles happen. So many, that politicians, on many occasions, should be called saints. Is it not true?" She smiled maliciously.

"Come on, Pedrina, not this time. You always get what you want, but this time it's absolutely impossible. I'm in a very tight spot. The municipal expenses have reached the maximum this year. Maybe next year. We'll talk about that on another occasion," he said, indicating that the meeting was over. And probably, it would have been, if he had not been talking to Aunt Pedrina.

"Correia, I know you want to be re-elected," she said, very confidently, knowing that she was pulling the best trick from her bag. "Helping the underprivileged is one of the best campaign strategies. Especially when the underprivileged are children. It never fails. Doing only what is proper and possible is a job for the Conservative Party. They haven't won an election in ten years. Voters love to see a politician with a bleeding heart. Can you imagine the impact it will cause in a speech during your next campaign? 'I made an enormous sacrifice to help the poor children from Indian Creek. I rebuilt the schoolhouse so those kids could get an education. Children are our future. We must make some sacrifices to raise our future leaders.' Correia, you can't deny this will put a big feather in your cap."

Correia's smile was so big that he could have bitten his two ears at the same time. "Wow! Pedrina, you have to promise to write some of my speeches for my next campaign." But he didn't think those speeches were going to be cheap. "How much money are we talking about? Remember, I'm in a very, very difficult position."

"First of all, I will help you with your speeches. I heard you in the last campaign. You do need help. Now, let's talk about the money we need to rebuild the schoolhouse; it won't be that much. I'm going to get people to volunteer for the labor. I already have promises of donations of building materials from various businesses. All the adults from Indian Creek signed up for volunteer work. Everyone is excited with this project. It's my intention to involve everyone."

"Pedrina, you are making me very nervous. I know your style, all this small talk is to cushion the big blast. No more small talk. How much money do you need for the job?"

"OK, OK. I estimate we need about twenty-five thousand. There, no need to panic. Only twenty-five."

"Twenty-five thousand! I'm sorry, this is way too much. I have no condition to raise this amount. Impossible!"

"Correia, consider the enormous benefit your campaign is going to gain. Twenty-five thousand is a bargain. You can't afford to miss this opportunity. I will bet that Moraes from the Conservative Party would give his own money for the project to impress the community. I'm sure he would make a good use of that in his campaign. Just imagine the impact when he says that you did not give the money to rebuild the schoolhouse because the people in Indian Creek are poor, not important, and they don't bother to go vote anyway. That will get him elected, you can be sure of that."

"Now, that's not fair. Pedrina, you're playing dirty tricks. It isn't fair; it's blackmail. You wouldn't give Moraes this opportunity. Would you?"

"Correia, I'm going to be honest with you. I want that schoolhouse finished for the next school year. I will not stop trying to get the money for the project. And I will get it any way I can. If I have to talk to Moraes, I will. I came to you first because I like you and I want to see you re-elected. (There she went again.) But you must realize it is a noble cause. It is something everybody in the community is going to talk about for a long time. This will be considered heroic. The only thing we have to decide is who is going to be the hero. It's up to you."

"Pedrina, you're impossible. If you ever decide to run for mayor, I won't run against you. You're too much. O.K., O.K. I will give you the money, but I want lots of publicity. I want my picture taken with the children from Indian Creek at every phase of the work."

"You've got it. We will place a sign saying: 'A humanitarian project of Mayor Correia. The mayor who works for all the people.' How about that?"

"Excellent! Pedrina, you're a political genius. You should be the manager of my campaign. The money will be available next week."

"Thanks, Correia. You will never regret this. I guarantee that helping those kids from Indian Creek will be the greatest accomplishment of your public life. And, by the way, you don't have to worry. I'll never run for mayor. For president . . . maybe. Who knows?"

They both laughed and she left his office walking tall and with her head up, flashing a victorious smile. She had been almost sure she'd be able to influence him to give what she wanted. It wouldn't be the first time; they had grown up around each other. However, it was a bit easier than she had expected. Maybe she was too conniving. But that was all right. Indeed, it was for a good cause.

Five

Pedrina in Action

Between practicing paddling her canoe back and forth across the river, recruiting volunteers for the construction, registering new students, and convincing farmers that sending their children to school was the right thing to do, she only had time to eat and sleep.

One of the things she did that was difficult, to say the least, but she found great pleasure in doing, was practicing her skills in handling a canoe. Aunt Pedrina's house was located not too far from the west bank of the river. At that point, the distance from one side to the other was about five hundred yards; the eastern shore was located a few miles from the Goat's Hill. Every morning the summer sun appeared first at the top of the small hill to shine upon the green waters of the river. The early morning hour on the river gave Aunt Pedrina, literally, a fresh, cool start for the day. When Juca and she arrived for the paddling training, the sun was also starting to come out from behind the hill and slowly begin to light up the sky and touch the western margin of the river. The eastern margin had a later start because it was covered by the shade projected from the hill standing in the way of the sunlight for a short time in the early morning. However, gradually the sunlight shimmering upon the surface of the water would broaden toward the east. In the early morning only reflections of sunlight were able to shine over the hill, pass through the woods, and gently brush some light from the middle of the river to the east bank. The western bank was where Aunt Pedrina started her practice.

By the time she finished the crossing, the sun had reached the eastern bank, making the river look like a crisp, golden mirror. The monotony of the sound of the oar diving repeatedly into the water had a soothing effect, giving her the opportunity to collect the energy she needed to face the day. But Aunt Pedrina loved challenges. The fact that the sun reached the other side before she did stimulated her spirit of competition. Encouraged by Juca, she tried hard to beat the sun across the river. Every morning she raced against the sun. The day she accomplished her goal, they had a loud and happy celebration. They sat on a stone on the bank and waited for the sun to arrive. Juca promoted her to full-fledged, first class canoewoman. The next thing, he figured, was to convince her to compete against him in fishing for the best catch.

That afternoon walking home, she was proud of her accomplishments, especially her victory over the sun. Suddenly, she wished to share her excitement with someone and realized how very lonely she was. Sadness overshadowed that happy moment. But just for a brief moment, she could almost feel Uncle Luiz's presence. A soft smile chased the sadness away and dried the tear that had begun to roll down her face. The soft smile became a big one and she started to walk fast and firm towards home.

Gramma was right. Everyone in the little town was talking about Aunt Pedrina. They were talking about the paddling, about the school, about her courage, and her dedication and determination in helping the children of Indian Creek. They were talking about everything. But, Gramma was not right about one thing: no one said she was not a lady. On the contrary, everyone was saying what a great lady she was.

Of course, Gramma heard all the talk. She was proud of her little sister. She loved to talk about Aunt Pedrina with her friends. "Times are changing," she would say, smiling. "Maybe society one of these days will recognize that women are much more capable than they get credit for. We'll see. . . ."

One Sunday morning she decided to go to see Aunt Pedrina and eat crow. It wasn't easy. Those two sisters were tough sisters. After the nine o'clock mass, she got one of her famous orange cakes, freshly baked, and went to visit her no less famous little sister.

"Dona Pedrina, Dona Pedrina. Dona Alice is here, she wants to talk with you," called Olinda, obviously anxious and a little agitated.

"Calm down, Olinda. She is only my sister, for God's sake. Tell her where I am and ask her to come in, she knows the house," Aunt Pedrina said casually without moving. Only her mouth and eyes moved gently, tugged subtly by a rascally smile.

"Good morning, Pedrina," Gramma said cautiously and a little bit uncomfortably. "How are you?"

"Good morning, Alice. I'm fine, thanks. How are you doing? What brings you to this 'no lady's' house?" Aunt Pedrina could be cold-hearted if it was necessary.

"Oh, Pedrina, stop! Don't be mean. You know that everything I said was to protect you. You're my sister. I love you and I don't want to see you hurt yourself. But . . . I was wrong. I'm sorry! Like everyone in town, I'm very impressed with your accomplishments. Can you forgive your older sister?" Gramma pleaded, making an exaggerated expression of innocence. "I brought an orange cake as a peace pipe."

"Of course I can, and I will. I know you love me and you didn't want to hurt me. However, sometimes you are a little snobby or, should I say, very snobby," Aunt Pedrina's naughty look slowly transformed into a welcoming smile. "I forgive you. Give me a big hug."

"Pedrina, I'm really sorry. I should know you would never do anything foolish."

"Listen, all this is in the past; let's forget it. Everything that was said and done was motivated by our best intentions, although sometimes good intentions can create bad feelings. Let's forget it and go to the kitchen and 'smoke' that orange peace pipe with a good cup of fresh coffee."

"You can't imagine the satisfaction of talking with you again. Talking, not screaming." Both of them laughed. "You're a very special sister. Thanks."

"You know, Alice, now that we're best friends again, I could use some help. I know you haven't taught for many years, but it's like riding a bicycle. You never forget. Since you're doing nothing besides baking orange cakes, what about coming to teach in Indian Creek with me?"

"Oh, no! You're not going to get me in that canoe of yours. You get Afonso to build a new bridge nearby and I'll think about going to teach with you."

They both laughed again. Aunt Pedrina and Gramma were good friends as well as sisters and truly loved each other. When Gramma passed away many years later, Aunt Pedrina told me it was the second saddest day of her life.

The schoolhouse in Indian Creek was a complete success. Due to the great response from the community, with very generous donations of money and building materials and the volunteer work, it was possible to build an addition on the back of the school. In this addition, they prepared accommodations for two extra teachers from out of town. Aunt Pedrina got the whole family and all her friends involved. She contacted many of her classmates from the Normal School and everyone made donations of books for the school library. In no time they had a school that the whole community was proud of.

She had some students that, when they finished their studies at Indian Creek, went to the town middle school and high school. Some got scholarships and went to the National University. Well, this is another story; I'll tell you later.

Aunt Pedrina was the principal, but she never shied away from other jobs, nor restricted herself to the principal's office. Because most of the work was done by volunteers, she liked to give moral support and assistance whenever someone came to help. She also decided to teach one class. The kids loved her; she touched them the same way she had touched us, with much love, understanding, and determination. She made them believe they could do or be anything they wanted, if they worked hard and focused on what they planned to do. A group of ladies from Indian Creek adopted the school and helped with the work. Even the new teachers were energized by the contagious enthusiasm. In a short time, the Indian Creek Grammar School was a landmark.

Six

A Lasting Impression

All these things I'm telling you, especially about the Indian Creek schoolhouse, happened many years before I was born. I learned all about it from the family, some family friends, and Aunt Pedrina herself. I was very young when I saw Aunt Pedrina for the first time. She was no longer teaching at the school, but she never stopped being an educator.

I became fascinated by her presence. There was something intriguing and challenging about her. She was kind always, and intimidating sometimes. I loved to watch and listen to her when she talked with Gramma, where I spent much time while I was growing up. I was raised by my aunt and uncle who traveled a great deal on business. When the trip was too long, I used to stay with Gramma. I felt a mixture of curiosity and fear about Aunt Pedrina. She was an impressive lady. I thought she was very tall when I first met her. But as I got older, I realized that she wasn't very tall. I was the one who was very little.

I remember when I was about seven years old, during one of my stays with Gramma, I asked her why Aunt Pedrina wore the same dress all the time. Gramma laughed. She told me they were not the same dress, they just looked alike. Aunt Pedrina used to buy a big roll of fabric and had the dressmaker make several dresses from the same roll of fabric, in the same style. The fabric was always black or navy blue, printed with tiny, white geometric designs or flowers. The style was simple: short sleeves with beehive stitches that made them look fluffy. The skirt was straight down to the ankles and had a very low V neckline. Everyone used to talk about Aunt Pedrina's low-cut dresses. One time I heard Gramma commenting that the neckline was a little too much. She suggested that some nice lace could be used to fill up the V. Pedrina paid no attention. She was not the type who would make any changes to please others. The low cut stayed low until she died and Aunt Dolores and cousin Lucia covered it with daisies.

Her gray hair was pulled back and tied in a little bundle with a flower finishing the design, usually an African daisy or a small spray of wildflowers. She had a contagious smile and when she spoke to me, animated with love and life, it would cause me to smile, too. She had a great sense of humor. She was the best storyteller I have ever known. But her appearance was not the most impressive thing about her. The genuine desire to understand and help others, her compassion and integrity, were the reasons people remembered her.

Because she wore the same style of dress, made from the same kind of fabric, don't think she was against changes and didn't know the latest fashion. She was very "avant-garde" in her own way. When the girls came to visit, she would comment on what they wore. She knew if they were up-to-date with the new fashion or not.

One time I heard her saying to cousin Lucia, "I didn't see you wearing anything in shocking pink. I understand it's the color for this season. And, your hair, according to Courrege, the French designer, should be very short in the back and the front should be a little longer pointing toward your chin. I think it would look attractive on you." For the boys, she wanted longer hair, an influence of the Beatles. She had a collection of LPs and many of them were from the Beatles. She said they would be classics one day.

She was an avid reader. She had subscriptions to many different newspapers and magazines from the capital and from around the world. She would read all the bestsellers. She was careful not to limit herself to one way of thinking. She read the conservative writers as well as the liberal. She was interested in all different opinions. "In order to learn," she used to say, "we must expose ourselves to many different concepts. Our responsibility is to analyze, understand, and digest what we have read, then draw our own conclusion in deciding what was right. You read, you learn."

She also said that when we limit our exposure to one opinion, it isn't learning, it's brainwashing. She told us over and over not to reject a new idea just because it's new or it comes from someone you don't know or don't like or disagree with. Listen to everything carefully with an open mind. There is a possibility this new idea could very well be the confirmation of your own convictions.

Her studio was in a bright room on the first floor of her house. It had two windows on the east side, which gave passage to the morning sun that usually traveled in company with a soft, constant breeze. Every single wall was covered with bookshelves full of books, papers, and magazines. In the far right corner, close to the south window, she had a small antique desk with a marble top. That was her reading and writing place. On the other side of the room was a comfortable stuffed chair, upholstered with green velvet, now faded, showing how much it had been used. This was my favorite spot. On her writing desk, she placed a small, crystal vase, very delicate, always with a colorful bouquet of fresh wildflowers.

I spent many hours in that room talking with her, actually, mostly listening to her. I learned a lot from Aunt Pedrina: mathematics, geography, grammar, language, among other things, but most importantly, I learned about life. She never gave an opinion about anything claiming it to be the only or the best opinion on that particular subject. She would say, "Well, this is my opinion. You must get a second and, if possible, a third, so you can form your own."

I loved visiting with her. In Aunt Pedrina's house we never found cookies or cakes, like at Gramma's. Olinda and Aunt Pedrina were not much for baking, but we always found answers for our questions. Even when she didn't know the answer, she never let us down. She would say, "Well, I'm sorry I don't know the answer for this one, but we have so many books. One of them must have the answer you're looking for. Let's find out." And we always did.

After her retirement, Aunt Pedrina stayed very much at home. She was not the type to travel. However, she could tell you about the changes in the traffic in Paris, who won and who lost elections around the world, the latest scientific discoveries, and who was who in Hollywood. It was amazing how much information she had. Although she lived in a little town in the middle of nowhere, she had a tremendous appetite for living and learning. She wanted to be counted, she wanted to be an integral part of the circle of life.

The whole family, especially Gramma, was concerned that she lived alone. They thought she was too isolated. Little did they know. Aunt Pedrina was part of all the kids' lives. She was part of the excitement, frustration, and dreams we had; she guided and helped us accomplish our goals. And, when things didn't go well, she helped us overcome our disillusionment and failures. She was with us when we collected the broken pieces of our effort and tried again.

Seven
Olinda

She also had the company and loyalty of Olinda, who was completely dedicated to her. When Olinda came to work as a housekeeper, they both were very young. Uncle Luiz thought Aunt Pedrina didn't know much about keeping a house so he hired Olinda to help her, as well as to teach her about domestic engineering.

What Uncle Luiz didn't know, and probably never learned, was that Olinda knew only as much as Aunt Pedrina did. They had to learn together, not only housekeeping, but to be good friends, and indeed they learned. In the beginning, Olinda was the housekeeper and Aunt Pedrina was the lady of the house. The first time Olinda did the laundry, Aunt Pedrina told me, she had no idea how to do it. She placed a red towel in the tub to soak, and when she finished, Uncle Luiz had a bunch of pink socks and underwear. They had to learn everything.

But as the time went by, they didn't just learn their chores, they grew up and then grew old together. Olinda was always there, on happy days as well as on sad ones. When I got to be part of Aunt Pedrina's life, I became also part of Olinda's. They were two fine, mature women helping each other. Aunt Pedrina taught Olinda how to read and write and was responsible for Olinda's reading habit. They spent so much time reading, talking, and laughing together that many times they finished what the other had started to say. That was the way they lived for a long time.

Aunt Pedrina told me that when Olinda first came, dinner in the house was simple, very simple. They were miles away from the point where they could be considered gourmet chefs. In fact, I don't believe they ever got there. One day, they decided to prepare a special dinner for Uncle Luiz's birthday; they wanted to surprise him, and they sure did. They decided to prepare a roasted chicken, stuffing, gravy, and all the trimmings. They knew what they had to prepare, but they had no idea how to start. Aunt Pedrina asked Gramma, who was a good cook, for instruction. Gramma told her to go the butcher and order a large chicken, good for roasting. She said they would kill and clean the chicken for her.

What she had to do after that was simple: prepare a marinade sauce with salt; garlic; pepper; a tablespoon of tarragon; a tablespoon of rosemary; a small onion, chopped; and a bottle of good, dry, white wine. Joaquim, the grocer, would recommend the right wine. She told them to pound the garlic, salt, and pepper together, and then mix the resulting paste with the wine, the onion, and the herbs. Marinate the chicken for at least three hours. It's best when you let the chicken sleep in the wine overnight. Remove the chicken from the marinade sauce and scrape it clean of all spices. Then, place the chicken in the oven, pre-heated to 350 degrees, for about two hours, depending on the size of the bird, or until it was nice and golden. Gramma told them everything, how to make the stuffing, the gravy, what kind of vegetables, and, of course, how to decorate the plate. She even told Aunt Pedrina, "You must eat with your eyes first. Everything has to look beautiful."

What Gramma never told them, however, was to remove what was inside of the chicken. When Olinda brought the food to the table, the chicken looked delicious, they were proud of their culinary expertise. But when Uncle Luiz tried to cut the chicken, the gizzards, neck, feet, and everything else inside the golden chicken came out on the plate. First, Aunt Pedrina was in state of shock, staring at the platter full of chicken pieces and innards. After Uncle Luiz realized what the novice chefs had done, he bit his lip and looked sideways at Aunt Pedrina. Then they all had a good laugh. And unsure of what other disagreeable discoveries may be awaiting them, they decided to go out for dinner.

Well, not everyone was entertained by the chicken fiasco and had a good laugh. Olinda was embarrassed. She cleaned the table, hid in the kitchen, and had a good cry. But the big fiasco was Olinda's best cooking lesson. She learned the secrets, improved the recipe, and became famous for making the best roasted chicken in the family.

The next morning, Aunt Pedrina complained to Gramma about her faulty recipe. Gramma got angry because Aunt Pedrina blamed her for the disaster. "For God's sake, Pedrina, I can't believe you're that naïve. It's elementary. Everyone knows you have to clean the chicken inside and remove everything before you roast it."

"No, Alice, it is not so elementary. You told me the butcher would kill and clean the chicken for me. And now, you know at least two people who did not know that we must clean the inside of the chicken, Olinda and me. I'm sure we are not the only ones." From this day on, every time Aunt Pedrina asked Gramma for a recipe or any other thing about housekeeping, she would add, "Now, tell me about all the elementary and obvious things." They would always have a good laugh. The chicken fiasco became a family joke. In time, even Olinda ended up getting a kick out of it.

Eight
No Bad Seeds

When I was growing up, my cousins and I used to spend part of the school summer vacation at Gramma's farm, which was a coffee farm. Usually, our parents organized a group of us of about the same age to go together. Gramma lived in town, but the farm was not too far away. We all liked to go there. It had horses, cows, pigs, chickens, ducks, goats, and other domestic animals. We would go horseback riding, swim in the river, play games, and, in between, work at some chores.

Next to the main house was a fenced area with lots of fruit trees. One of our jobs was to care for the kitchen orchard. It was easy to grow a great variety of fruit trees in the rich soil and tropical climate. There were persimmons, peaches, carombola, and cashew fruit. Citrus trees grew well and Gramma was always loaded with oranges and limes. Grapefruit was also easy to raise, but neither Gramma nor the farm workers liked it. The cousins and I would rake leaves, remove dead branches from the ground, and fix the wood fence where it was needed. They were simple kid jobs but the good part was we got paid every Saturday.

Gramma used to say that we should save our money for when we went back to school. We thought that was funny because we really had little choice, there was no place to spend money on or anywhere near Gramma's farm.

Aunt Pedrina used to stay at the farm with us during our vacation to be company for Gramma and help to keep an eye on the kids. The truth of the matter was, she was company for us and kept an eye on Gramma.

I remember one summer when the temperature was not the only thing that was hot. Our temperaments were even hotter. We had always gotten along fine, but that particular summer, for some reason, we were awfully disagreeable. We were fighting over everything or nothing, no matter how foolish it was. One afternoon, Aunt Pedrina called everybody to the veranda. She had a small flowerpot full of soil and three grains of corn. She opened the soil in the middle, put the three grains in, covered them with soil, and put some water over them.

"Does everyone know what I just did?" she asked seriously, which was strange for a person who was always smiling.

"You planted three grains of corn," we answered, quite sure of ourselves.

"O.K., you can go now," she told us, waving us away with her hands. She looked concerned.

All the kids became suspicious. We knew her well, so we knew she was cooking something up and whatever it was, we were going to eat it, whether we liked it or not.

We continued arguing, fighting, and being disagreeable. We forgot all about the corn in the little pot until a week or ten days after our encounter on the veranda, when she called everyone back .We knew something was going to take place. She had the same pot, or one that looked like it. The only difference was that now the flowerpot had three little green sprouts about three inches tall. We knew then, this meeting was related to the first one, we just didn't know how. She looked everyone in the eyes and asked, continuing very seriously, "I believe all of you know what these green sprouts are?"

We felt uneasy; we were afraid we might give the wrong answer. I told you she could be intimidating sometimes. No one wanted to say anything. All of us hoped someone else would answer so we could get out from there fast. My cousin, Paulo, the oldest of the bunch, answered in a squeaky voice; he was so nervous, his voice would not come out. "Co . . . corn. I believe it's a corn plant."

"Right. It is a corn plant, a very small one. You and everyone else know this because you saw me planting the three grains of corn. I planted corn and now I have a corn plant. Life works on the same principle; it is like this little pot. You get from life exactly what you put into it. I plant corn, I'm going to get corn. Lately, all of you have been putting too much hostility, disagreement, rudeness, and bad attitude in your little 'pot' and that is what all of you have been getting from each other, hostility, disagreement, rudeness, and bad attitude. When we go through life spreading negative and unpleasant behavior, we have to prepare ourselves because that is exactly what we can expect to get in return.

"If all of you spend time helping and being friendly to each other, you could have a wonderful summer, a vacation that could become a pleasant memory. You are wasting precious time. Think about what I just said. You can go now. And please plant these three little plants in a sunny place." She did not look happy and, again, she waved us out.

We left slowly and quietly. I'm not sure how much impact that demonstration had on everyone then. I don't even remember if there was any change in behavior among us. But one thing I'm absolutely sure of, I never forgot what she told us, "We get from life what we put into it." What happens in our life is, in many instances, a reflection of our actions. Many times in my adult life I made decisions based on this principle. I try to have a positive attitude, to avoid planting any bad seeds that could germinate into unpleasant situations.

Nine
Getting Even

Aunt Pedrina had an intrinsic determination to make the world a better place and, always, was prepared to help someone who needed help. She used to tell us that when God created this world, He provided it with everything we need, enough for everyone. We just have to learn how to share.

Scores of people in that little town would not make any serious decision without talking to her first and getting her opinion. They trusted her judgment. Because she read so much on such a diversity of subjects, they came to her with all kinds of problems such as legal questions, tax questions, how to write a will, or how to read and understand a contract. She was actually practicing law without a license, but that was O.K.; everyone knew she wasn't a lawyer and she never charged a fee.

It doesn't make any difference where we live or what language we speak, we can find people willing and capable of taking advantage of others; people who have no scruples and are willing to benefit from the ingenuity of others. Aunt Pedrina's little town was no exception. They had a few, and one of them made her very annoyed. His name was Carlito de Melo, a dishonest real estate agent who would prey on old ladies and widows or anyone who did not have much business experience. He would trick them into selling their properties for almost nothing, and he, in turn, would resell them for much more, making a big profit. He knew how to manipulate people to believe and trust him. He was a fast-talker who knew all the tricks in the encyclopedia of dirty deals.

Aunt Pedrina had a good piece of land that Carlito was pestering her to sell to him. She knew the way he operated and avoided any contact with him. But he would not give up. Persistence was a strategy he used successfully. He kept calling. But remember what I told you, she was a good teacher, so she decided to teach him a lesson he would never forget.

One afternoon, she invited two of her good friends to come to her house for an afternoon coffee. She also invited Carlito to come, but did not tell her friends that he would be there also.

When he arrived, she and her friends were having coffee. Casually, like their presence was just a coincidence, she invited him to sit down. "Oh, Mr. Carlito, thank you for coming. These are my good friends, Mrs. Maria Vieira and Mrs. Rosa Campos. Would you like to join us and have some coffee?" Maria and Rosa were shocked at seeing Carlito de Melo in Aunt Pedrina's house. They knew his reputation; they couldn't understand why Aunt Pedrina had invited that man into her home when she had told them to avoid him and never, under any circumstance, do any business with him.

"That's very nice, Dona Pedrina. Yes, thank you." He sat down and Olinda gave him coffee and cake. Olinda was quiet and had a mysterious half grin. She was part of the plan.

Aunt Pedrina began to explain Carlito's presence to her friends, "Mr. Carlito wants to buy the land I have next to the gas station. I'm considering selling it to him. That land is nothing but trouble. I have no intention to build anything, but I have to have someone keep the land clean all the time. If I don't keep it clean, the city will send me a citation, and if I don't clean it immediately after that, I'll be fined. It doesn't make any sense for me to keep the land. The maintenance is getting too expensive. My luck is that Mr. Carlito wants to buy it and free me from this trouble."

Maria and Rosa were even more confused. Why did Aunt Pedrina want to do business with this man? They knew she detested and didn't trust him, and had warned them about him. Neither said much. They were uncomfortable, and sat tensely at the edge of their chairs. They picked distractedly at their cake as a bird cautiously keeps watch of its surroundings as it pecks at an early morning meal.

"I'll be happy to help you, Dona Pedrina," he said. "You've done so much for this community, you deserve a carefree life now. I think you are making the right decision."

"So, you're sure I should sell the land?" she asked, pretending innocence. "And how are you going to do that? Are you going to put the land on the market and advertise it for sale?" she said, broadening her performance.

"Answering your first question," he replied professionally, "yes, you should sell. Now, as far as putting it on the market and advertising, yes, I'm going to do that right away. But, you know, maybe I will not find a buyer immediately. However, I'm going to make it easy for you. I'll buy it from you and then sell it. This way we save your time. You won't have to worry anymore about cleaning the lot and you'll have the cash to invest or spend immediately."

"But, Mr. Carlito," cautioned Aunt Pedrina, still playing 'poor little me,' "you're going to tie up your capital without knowing when you will be able to recoup it. That isn't right."

"Oh, Dona Pedrina, don't concern yourself with that. I've been in the real estate business for a long time. My job is buying and selling properties. I do this all the time. What kind of price do you have in mind for the land?" Carlito asked, trying to change the conversation.

"Oh well, I'm not sure." Aunt Pedrina paused thoughtfully, pretending not have any business experience. "I thought I could get ten thousand. Do you think it would be a fair price?" She was good . . . very good.

Carlito sat upright, his expression full of pity and sadness, "Oh, Dona Pedrina, I'm sorry, ten thousand is too high. The real estate market is not good right now, especially empty lots. You would never be able to get that much for the land. I have a nice piece of land by the creek. I'm asking five thousand and I'm having trouble selling. Land is not going too high these days."

"I see," Pedrina said, "I know the land you're talking about. It is a good piece of land. I thought it would go for much more than that."

"No. I'm trying to get five thousand, but I can't find a buyer," Carlito complained in a fake, painful whine.

Aunt Pedrina's eyes were bright. Carlito had bitten. Smirking, she said slowly, "Well, Mr. Carlito, I think I can help you. I'm going to give you a check for five thousand. I will instruct my attorney to take the legal steps to transfer the title to my name."

Carlito de Melo jumped in the air like a mad goat. He was red like a ripe tomato, his eyes wide open. He looked like he was going to explode. He started to walk around the table, with his hands in the air, repeating, like a mad man, "This is ridiculous, this is ridiculous! You told me you wanted to sell your land, not buy my lot. This is ridiculous, this is ridiculous! You set me up."

Looking very cool and collected, revealing a Mona Lisa

smile, she said, "Yes, Mr. Carlito de Melo, I set you up, and if you back out of this deal I have two witnesses and I will take you to court. I may not get that beautiful piece of land for five thousand. You may be able to fight back because we don't have a written contract. But, you can be sure I will make you lose your real estate license because of your unethical business practice. You will no longer be able to exploit old ladies in this town. Olinda, go and bring the police."

Carlito ran out of the house. He was afraid Olinda would come back with the police and he would be in bigger trouble. Maria and Rosa could not stop laughing.

"Pedrina, you are incredible," said Maria. "For a moment you had us fooled. Rosa and I were so distressed by the possibility you would allow Carlito to take advantage of you. You're too much. You deserve the Oscar for best performance of the year."

"I was just letting him hang himself with his own rope," Aunt Pedrina explained. "I had talked with several people whom he had tricked before I invited him to my house. They didn't file an official complaint or talk to anyone about it because they were embarrassed for being so naïve. I was well aware of his strategy." Olinda came back from the kitchen where she had been hiding, pretending she had gone for the police. She also was laughing excitedly.

"Olinda, I think all of us, including you, need more coffee and more of my sister's famous orange cake. She probably is dying of curiosity to know how the meeting was with Carlito. She and Olinda were the only ones who knew about my plan," she said to Maria and Rosa. Coffee and Gramma's cake never tasted so good.

Aunt Pedrina never forced Carlito to sell the land to her for five thousand. She never pressed the issue. She didn't want to do to him the same thing he had done to others. However, she did file suit against his unethical behavior. The Board of Realtors canceled his license after an investigation. Shortly after the incident, he left town forever. He had no future there.

Ten

Identity Crisis

Aunt Pedrina had a natural ability to discover those who needed help. She was alert to people's pain and ready to fight to protect someone in need. She would not allow any one of us to be abused or disrespected by others, nor would she allow us to abuse or disrespect others. Youngsters, many times, can be cruel, not necessarily because they are bad, but because they think they are being funny. She fought for the underdog. I had a personal experience of that kind.

I was about twelve years old. As usual, all the kids were spending part of school vacation on Gramma's farm. One Saturday morning, Aunt Dolores came to get all the kids to go to town. The only movie theater was showing *The Yellow Submarine* with the Beatles. I decided not to go with them. When Aunt Pedrina saw me, she looked surprised. "How come you're here? I thought everybody went to see the movie."

"I didn't go," I said coldly, hoping it would be the end of that conversation.

"Why not?" she asked. Aunt Pedrina was not a person you could easily push aside.

"I didn't want to go. I don't want to go anywhere with them, ever again." The way I answered, it was obvious I was angry for some reason. This was sufficient to make her interested in what had happened between my cousins and me. A twelve-year-old boy would not miss *The Yellow Submarine* with the Beatles unless there was a serious motive, for him, anyway.

"Why?" she asked, examining carefully my expression, trying to read what I was not verbally communicating.

"I want to stay home."

"Come on," Aunt Pedrina tried coaxing more information from me, "You're too smart to think I'd believe that. I thought we were friends and we trusted each other. I didn't think we kept secrets between us."

She was right. I knew I could trust her. She was not just my friend, she was the best friend anyone could ever have. Besides, I was hurt and angry. I needed someone to talk to. I didn't think there was anyone better qualified.

"I don't want ever to do anything with them. They keep calling me Indian. They said I was born in the jungle in an Indian tribe, where everyone walks around naked. I know that isn't true, but I'm tired of it. They keep saying this over and over. I don't want to be around them anymore. I want to go home."

"I understand how you feel. It's dreadfully annoying when someone keeps repeating something, no matter how stupid. But they keep doing that because they get you angry. And that's exactly what they want. As long as they get the result they want, they will continue. For them it's like a game. You and I have to develop a strategy to force them to stop. But before we decide what we're going to do, we have to put everything into perspective. Let's organize all the facts. The real ones. Do you understand?"

"No. I don't know what you mean by the real facts," I said. "What they are saying is not true. It isn't a real fact.

Right?" I asked, a little uneasy. I was kind of nervous, I was afraid she would say something I wouldn't like to hear.

Aunt Pedrina looked through me, seeming to be evaluating her words carefully, trying to guess how I would react. It was like she was going to reveal a secret, but was not sure if she should do it. "Don't worry about it. I'm going to help you understand everything. But you have to be patient and allow me time enough to organize my thoughts. First of all, you should not say you want to go home. You are home. This place is your home as much as it is their home. Your Gramma would be hurt if she knew you don't think this is your home. She loves all of you very much, the same way."

I stared at the floor and quietly replied, "Yes, I know."

"Now, let's consider the facts and see if they are real facts or unfounded rumors. Were you born in the jungle? No, you were not. This is not a real fact. I remember the day you were born. You were born in the Municipal Maternity, in the capital. Your Aunt Maria de Lurdes has all the papers. You can ask and she will show them to you and you can verify it.

"Next, are you an Indian? Well . . . yes and no. You are part Indian. Your maternal great-grandmother, your mother's grandmother, was one hundred percent Indian. Your grandmother was one half, your mother was one quarter. That makes you one-eighth Indian. But when you learn all the details, you will be one hundred percent proud of your origin.

"I didn't know your great-grandmother," she continued, "however, I had the pleasure of knowing your grandmother and I knew your mother very well; two very fine ladies of exceptional qualities. They were strong women and raised wonderful families. Unfortunately, they both died young. What do you know about your mother?"

"Not much," I said. "I just know she died when I was a few months old."

"I'm not sure, but some people will say I shouldn't tell you all this. They'll probably say you're too young and you don't have to know this now. But you're having an identity crisis. I want to help you. Do you know what an identity crisis is?" she asked.

"I think so," I said, very interested in everything she was saying. "Identity crisis. . . . I think it's when we are not sure of who we are. Right?" I was not sure, but by her reaction, I felt I had passed the identity crisis test.

"Right," Aunt Pedrina grinned proudly. After all, she was a part of my identity. "Very well. In order to understand who we are, and be proud of who we are, we must learn everything we can about ourselves. When your mother learned she was pregnant with you, she had passed the prime time for motherhood, plus she was not very healthy. Your oldest sister, Clara, was already married. The doctor didn't want your mother to carry the whole pregnancy; he suggested she should terminate it."

Our conversation was getting more and more interesting. I forgot I was angry with my cousins and missing *The Yellow Submarine.* I was in my own submarine, voyaging to places known yet unknown, exploring the history of me. Aunt Pedrina continued with my story.

"Your mother's only concern was that if the baby was to be born, would he or she be well and in good health. When the doctor answered yes, she said, 'That's all I want to know. I'll have my baby.' She was a courageous and strong-willed woman. She loved her children. She died a few months after you were born. Since your Aunt Maria de Lurdes is the younger sister of your mother and married to my younger nephew, who is your father's brother, your father let her raise you. She never had any children of her own. She loves you very much and has been your mother since the day you were born. Did you know all that?"

"I knew some, not all, of the details. I didn't know my mother could not have more children. No one ever told me that."

"Adults sometimes choose to keep secrets from children," Aunt Pedrina explained, softly touching my shoulder and pulling me next to her. "They usually underestimate the ability of children to understand what they consider adult things. They keep secrets, even when the secret doesn't belong to them, but belongs to the children. They think they are protecting the child. They create cushions around the child to hide the truth. Sometimes those cushions become hard, like rocks, with sharp edges, and they can wound and cause scars that last forever."

"Why do they do that, if it is not good for the child?" I asked.

"I don't know. Maybe, in the process of growing up, some of us lose our innocence and many pure and beautiful feelings. We become wary, confused by countless complications and then unable to grasp and express emotions we could, easily, when we were young." Everything she was saying, the details of my birth and my origin, were capturing my attention. However, I was having some problem connecting it all with my identity crisis.

"Now, about your great-grandmother. How did you get a full-blooded Indian for a great-grandmother? (Oh, oh, I think we are going to enter into the phase of my crisis.) It happened a long time ago. A married couple from Portugal, Helena and Henrique, were visiting our country. He was an anthropologist and was conducting a study about a particular Brazilian Indian tribe's culture and life. Henrique's university, which organized and was supervising the studies, provided them with a guide who, besides speaking the tribe's language, knew about their customs and culture. He was assigned to assist the professor.

"They were visiting an Indian village when Helena noticed a young Indian woman with an infant who was no more than two months old. The professor and his wife did not have any children. They were unable to have a child, but they wanted to have a baby very much. For some time, they had been thinking about adoption. Helena was absolutely fascinated with the baby. She asked the guide about the possibility of a couple from Europe adopting an indigenous infant. The guide told her that he had no information about it. He had no recollection of any adoption. He suggested that the best way would be to ask the Indian woman about it before inquiring about the legality of it.

"Helena was very excited with the possibility. She instructed the guide about what to say. She asked him to inform the young woman that if they adopted a baby, the child would be taken to Portugal, where they were from, and the baby would have the opportunity of a comfortable life, education and security. They would treat the child as their own and would do everything possible to provide to their son or daughter a very happy life.

"The conversation between the guide and the young woman was disappointingly short. She became upset. She held the infant tightly against her chest and shook her head no, no. She turned the child to the other side, like she did not want them to see the baby anymore. At the same time she was repeating the same word in her dialect, continuing to shake her head. It was obvious to everyone the idea of adoption was not received well.

"Helena was concerned and started gesturing to the young woman to calm down. She asked the guide to tell the woman to please not to worry, they would not do anything against her will. She was sorry for upsetting the young mother. She didn't know what to do to calm the young Indian. She was sorry for creating a frightening and unpleasant situation for her. Helena and Henrique were considerate people.

"They continued their research in the village, asking questions and making notes and detailed drawings of the utensils and tools, to establish the kind of life in this remote part of the country, far away from any form of modern civilization. The young Indian woman sat down where she could follow them with her eyes, especially Helena.

"When it came time for lunch, Helena, Henrique, and the guide sat down to eat. Helena went to the car and brought back a basket of fresh fruits they had packed for the trip. The young Indian was interested in what Helena was doing. When she noticed that she was being observed, Helena prepared a plate and gave it to the guide to give to the young woman. She looked at it suspiciously. She smelled the fruits she was not familiar with. I guess she wanted to find out if they were poisonous. Indians are highly skillful in identifying things that can or cannot be eaten. She liked the smell. She ate some and saved the rest.

"After they finished eating, Helena placed the basket and the dishes back into the car and went with Henrique and the guide to another area of the village. After a short time, they came back. The young woman didn't look so scared anymore. Helena was tired and sat down to rest. The young Indian came to her without the baby and gave Helena a full hand of various wild berries. Helena ate some and made faces to the young Indian indicating she liked the berries. That was the first direct contact they had. The young woman smiled, covering her face with her hands. She was almost a child herself. The young woman continued observing Helena at short distance, so short that she noticed Helena's pearl necklace.

"The necklace was a gift from Henrique. Helena didn't feel comfortable leaving it in the hotel, so she put it inside the blouse to prevent it from being seen. The young Indian became curious and moved closer to take a better look. She could not resist touching the pearls, fascinated by the unusual shining whiteness and buttery smooth surface. Of course, she had never seen anything like them. Helena's necklace was magnificent, made of perfect pearls, all the same size and of a dazzling, rich luster. It would have caught the attention of any woman anywhere.

"Helena and Henrique continued their work, examining utensils, tools, weapons, anything that would help them finish their research. The young Indian was more comfortable with their presence, continuing to follow them at a short distance, but her eyes were fixed on Helena. She was interesting in everything Helena did, especially when Henrique and the guide spoke with Helena. It appeared the young mother was trying to establish and understand Helena's culture and way of life. The curiosity was mutual.

"After gathering all of the information they believed was needed for their research, they were getting ready to leave. The young Indian was very still, watching Helena intently. As a last attempt, Helena told the guide to tell the young Indian that if she gave the baby to her, she would give her to necklace. When the guide spoke with the young woman, there was a heavy silence, absolutely no movement, no reaction. She stood immovable, like her thoughts were thousands of miles away. After some time, Henrique told Helena that the young woman wasn't going to do it for any reason; she would not give up her child. He said it was getting too late. They had to go; it was a long trip back to the hotel. When they started to get into the car, the young Indian ran to get the baby and brought it to Helena. Helena took the necklace off and gave it to the young woman, who had an expression of sadness and anxiety. She held the necklace with both hands, pressing it against her belly, bending over like she was in pain, gazing at the baby with tears rolling down her face. The car started to move. Helena did not look back; she didn't have the courage. With an equally sad expression and tears in her eyes, she looked to the baby and said, 'They were real pearls, but you are much more precious.' The baby was a beautiful little girl who later became your great-grandmother. Helena and Henrique are your adoptive great-great-grandparents."

"But wait, Aunt Pedrina," I asked, "she exchanged the baby for the necklace just like that? Like it was not important?" I felt disappointed and uneasy about trading a thing, no matter how beautiful, for a person.

"I don't think so. In my opinion, the necklace was not the decisive factor in the exchange," Aunt Pedrina said, visibly emotional. "The young mother, was, probably, evaluating Helena's maternal instinct, the future of her daughter, and most of all, the promise of a better life. In some Indian tribes, when they had a big war against another tribe, the winners took whatever they wanted from the losers.

"Many times they would take the young girls to give as wives for the warriors. When the winners returned to their villages with their new wives, the women of their village treated the girls like slaves. They were forced to do all the work and most the time they were brutalized. A person does not have to be educated, sophisticated, or even civilized to recognize the importance of being treated with dignity and respect. The young Indian could have, very well, been one of the poor little girls given as a trophy for a victorious warrior. The promise of a safe and happy life for her baby girl was probably the most important factor. Much more important than the pearl necklace. There is also the possibility the young mother wanted her daughter to be just like Helena. And that was why she made the supreme sacrifice. I don't know . . . I'm not sure and probably never will be."

"This is an amazing story. How do you know all that?" I asked skeptically.

"Henrique and Helena were well-educated. They both were university professors. Because they were conducting anthropological research, they kept a journal with the details of the events of that day, as well as all the information about the tribe's life as part of their study. Helena made special notations regarding her interaction with the young mother.

"When they took your great-grandmother home, they made a special copy of all the events for her, including a map of the location of the tribe and its name. They also wrote down a lot of personal information about the little girl and her natural mother's origin. They wanted her to know everything about her background. Your great-grandmother made copies of the journal for her children; her children gave copies to their children, and so forth.

"That information has been passed from generation to generation. Your Aunt Maria de Lurdes has a copy, your sisters and brothers have one. They are probably waiting for you to get older to give you a copy. Your mother and I were good friends. She gave me one copy, which I read many times. I keep my copy in a safe place.

"Apparently, your cousins heard bits and pieces of the story. If they didn't know anything, they would not call you Indian. Well, this is your story. You have the right to know the whole thing. And the time for you to know, I believe, is right now."

"Thanks. It was nice of you. Now that I know the

whole story, it may not bother me as much if they call me Indian again," I said.

Aunt Pedrina looked at me with a naughty look and her famous Mona Lisa smile, "Now . . . when they call you Indian, you have to straighten them up. You have to say to them, they are not right. You are only one-eighth Indian. Your great-grandmother was a full-blooded Indian, but the family had to give a pearl necklace, made of real pearls, to get her to be part of the family. Then ask them what their family had to give to get their great-grandmothers."

Aunt Pedrina wrote to the National Indian Institute and gave them the information and the location of my great-grandmother's tribe. She told them about me and my story. She wanted to buy some artifacts made by my ancestors to give to me. They sent her an antique necklace made of small bones, very small feathers, and beads. She gave it to me for my birthday.

I was pleased with my Indian necklace and showed it to everyone. When I took it to my school, it was a big success. The interesting thing was that it took a pearl necklace to give my great-grandmother her European identity and an antique Indian necklace, made by my ancestors, to restore my Indian identity, of which I'm very proud. I felt special, and close to my mother and great-grandmother.

Eleven

To Your Health

Aunt Pedrina was a firm believer that for every action, there was a motivation to stimulate the action. She always tried to make us identify our motivation so we could decide if our action was acceptable. In the process, she made it possible for us to see things in a way we had never seen them before. She was not Pollyanna; she was a person with a great sense of reality. She knew pain, hope, deception, frustration, and success. She told us often that we all had the ability to overcome obstacles and increase our possibilities and opportunities if we trusted ourselves and worked hard. She was not a dreamer; she was an optimist.

Her generosity, wisdom, and sense of justice were for us like a grand mirror where we could see the reflection of our own image, making it possible for us to recognize and understand our flaws and qualities. She always tried to help us find the best way to become strong and sensitive at the same time. But she was not always so righteous and proper. Many times she did funny and naughty things. She loved to see us laugh, having a good time, being kids, doing kids' things. Occasionally, she would allow us to do things that, according to Gramma, were not right, much less appropriate.

Aunt Pedrina and Gramma were best of friends; however, they did not share the same opinion about a lot of things. From time to time, they disagreed about the best way to correct some of the kids' behavior. Gramma was strict; her life was guided by rules and regulations, no flexibility. Aunt Pedrina was more liberal. She used to tell us that we should be good people and never do anything to hurt anyone. Nevertheless, we should have fun and enjoy our youth and not take anything too seriously. Gramma was always disagreeing with the way Aunt Pedrina treated us. "Too much freedom," Gramma used to say, "too much freedom."

Gramma was like an army sergeant. We must pay attention to the rules and regulations; time to go to bed, time to get up, time to eat, what to eat, time to play, and how to play. When we were playing outside, we could hear her voice coming from somewhere, "You are not behaving like ladies and gentlemen."

We used to imitate Gramma and say to each other, "You are not behaving like ladies and gentlemen!" Of course, we were careful not to let her see or hear us doing that.

She used to say that in the city we didn't eat properly because there were too many places where we could eat things that weren't nutritious or appropriate for our ages. Her opinion was that we didn't eat enough fresh vegetables, fruits, and milk. While we were on the farm, every meal was a nutrition lesson. We had no problem with fresh vegetables and fruits—they were terrific—but the milk . . . that was an entirely different matter.

Antonio was the overseer. He was in charge of the other workers and ran the farm for Gramma. He was born on the farm. His father worked for my great-grandfather, from whom Gramma inherited the farm. When the kids were there on vacation, she gave him orders to bring a nice clean cow and tie it next to the house every morning. We had to get in line with an oversized mug and get milk straight from the cow. That was absolutely the worst part of our perfect nutrition. The milk, which was the cow's body temperature, smelled and tasted like a stable. Aunt Pedrina saw the disgusted look on our faces. She knew how much we hated to drink that milk.

She tried many times to convince Gramma she should not force us to drink milk that way. But Gramma was convinced it was for our own good and we would get used to it eventually. She didn't give in. No one could make her change her mind. Aunt Pedrina decided to take matters into her own hands. She bought a bottle of cocoa syrup, alcohol free. It was sweet and had a nice aroma, a delicious, chocolate taste. Every morning, without Gramma's knowledge, she put a little shot of syrup in everybody's mug. Oh, boy! We all started to look forward to the morning milk.

One morning, Gramma was watching us drinking the milk. She had a victorious smile and told to Aunt Pedrina, "You see, I told you they would get used to drinking fresh milk. If I'm not mistaken, I believe they've acquired a taste for it. That's very good for them in the growing age."

Aunt Pedrina was still, quietly composed. She looked at us with truth in the corner of her eyes, nodded her head affirmatively and, without facing Gramma said, "Hum hum!" Controlling herself so not to laugh, she walked away to avoid any more remarks about how much we liked the milk. We knew we had to rinse the mugs before we placed them on the countertop in the kitchen to destroy the evidence of the crime. The secret, the mystery, and the guilty feeling added to the flavor of the morning milk.

Twelve
A Scary Night

Rescuing us from our fears was another thing she was always ready to do. She had a unique way of explaining what was happening, why it was happening, and then giving us some options for how to deal with the problem, based on the reality of the situation, so as not to be totally lost to panic. She was teaching us to develop positive thinking and the ability to take initiative. She did not want us to become dependent on others. She always said it is perfectly all right to have help as long as we are an active participant in the problem-solving process.

All of us knew we could go to her any time we faced a situation we didn't know how to deal with. She had already taught us not to panic. It is important to maintain calm. The best way is to learn everything we can about the situation, so we can anticipate the implications. Then we can develop a strategy to solve the problem. She used to say, "Every problem, no matter how complicated it seems to be, has a solution, and most of the time, it's a simple one."

One night on the farm, I was awoken from a deep sleep by a strange sound. It was a soft noise, almost like people were chanting far away, in the form of a litany. I tried to listen to see if I could understand what they were saying, but it was too far away and was barely audible. I listened for a while and had the impression they were coming closer to the farm. I looked through a small crack in the window shutters of my bedroom, and I saw at a distance, a line of little lights, moving slightly up and down, coming slowly toward us. The sound seemed to be synchronized with the movement. I remember being frightened. I was young and had no idea what that strange noise could be. I didn't know what to do. My imagination was running wild, conjuring images of lumbering beasts or wavering ghostly wisps.

The house was deathly quiet; everyone resting peacefully. I sat on the edge of the bed and listened to the chanting that, definitely, was coming slowly yet persistently in our direction.

I had no idea about the time, but I thought it was late. It was dark and I felt cold; I wrapped myself with a blanket. Gramma's home was an old farmhouse with a large center room that combined living room, dining room, and family room. On the south side were the kitchen (a large one), a pantry, the washroom, and the maid's quarters. On the north side was the entrance hall, with a double door that opened to a large veranda. The north side was the front of the house. The bedrooms were located on the east and west wings. All the kids stayed in the east wing, with three large bedrooms and a small one that was my bedroom. Gramma and Aunt Pedrina stayed in the west wing. There were also three large bedrooms and a small room that was used as a sewing and ironing room. The house did not have electricity. A generator produced electricity for the kitchen (one light and the refrigerator) and a small chandelier over the dining room table. The rest of the house had individual oil lamps. Every night at 9 P.M. Antonio turned off the generator until 5 A.M. the next morning.

I wanted to call somebody, but not one of the kids. I wanted one of the adults, any one. I believed we were in the imminence of something frightfully serious and dangerous. It was urgent that Gramma or Aunt Pedrina be notified. The rooms were silent except for the noises that old houses make when cooling off after a hot, humid afternoon. The squeaks and groans of the old frame structure made the situation more sinister, increasing my panic. I listened, hoping someone would wake up. After painfully waiting for someone to come, I decided to wake up Gramma or Aunt Pedrina. I wrapped myself tightly with the blanket, like it was a shield, and opened my bedroom door. The center room appeared bigger than a football field. The silence was so loud it caused my ears to pound. I did not walk, I ran as fast as I could to Aunt Pedrina's room and started banging, frantically, on the door.

"Yes, who is that? Who is there? Yes, yes," she answered, awake, but not yet alert.

"Aunt Pedrina, it's me. Please, please open the door!" I cried.

"The door is not locked. Come in," she said. I rushed into the room at the velocity of a bullet and closed the door behind me. She was sitting on the edge of her bed, lighting an oil lamp. "Oh my goodness!" she said looking at me. "You look like you just saw a ghost. What's the matter with you? What happened?"

"Aunt Pedrina, there's something outside. I don't know what it is, but whatever it is, it's coming in this direction. I'm scared. I'm scared."

"Calm down, calm down." She pulled me into the softness of her flannel nightgown and stroked the back of my head. "Let's go and see what this thing is. I'm sure it's nothing but your imagination. You probably had a nightmare."

She lifted the lamp from the nightstand and we started moving toward my bedroom. By now, everybody was up. I had banged on Aunt Pedrina's door so hard, making so much noise, that every living thing in the house was running back and forth in the center room. Everyone was carrying a candle or a lamp, casting giant shadows that danced on the walls. The whole scene resembled the wailing, frantic characters of a horror movie fleeing from the unseen, frightened by the fear of the others. Aunt Pedrina alone held calm.

When we got into my room, we looked through the crack in the shutters. Some of the workers' houses had oil lights flickering in their windows. Aunt Pedrina held me and said, "Poor child, no wonder you were scared. It's a funeral."

"A funeral? In the middle of the night?" I asked in disbelief.

"Yes, a funeral. Antonio and some of the workers are already outside. Gramma and I have to go out, too. You kids stay in here. When they leave, we will have a cup of hot chamomile tea and I'll tell you all about it. There is no reason to be afraid."

After Gramma and Aunt Pedrina went outside, all the kids ran into my room. We cramped in on top of each other, pushing and shoving to take a peak through the crack in the window shutters to find out what was going on. Because they were close to the house, from my window we could see them and hear their voices. There were several people standing outside in a circle. Among them were Antonio, some of the workers, plus several people we didn't know. I believe they came with the funeral. They were talking softly, but we could hear what they were saying. There were two wooden sticks propped up, holding a hammock, which looked like someone was lying in it. Constancia, Antonio's wife, was passing around coffee and cake. Another worker arrived carrying a kerosene lamp. "Who died?" he asked, placing the lamp on the ground next to the hammock. The lamp on the ground projected a flickering light on everybody's faces, making the group eerily unearthly, almost like ghosts.

"An old man from Alegria, a small farm not far from here," someone answered.

"Was it murder or was he taken by God?"

"Tuberculosis," said a woman who was standing beside the hammock.

Gramma made the sign of the cross and said, "I'm sorry. May God bless his soul and give him eternal peace." She gave the envelope she had brought to the same woman; I think she was the dead man's daughter. The envelope had money. I knew it was money because I had seen Gramma and Aunt Pedrina put money in the envelope before they went outside.

Antonio brought his truck to the area where they were standing. They covered the truck bed with an old blanket and carefully placed the hammock inside. Everyone who came with the funeral got in the truck as well and started to light the candles they had been holding. As the truck drove off, we saw the lights become smaller and farther away until they were swallowed by the darkness of the night.

Olinda and Yolanda were making chamomile tea. Gramma believed chamomile tea was the best thing to calm down your nerves and put you to sleep.

When they got back inside, we sat in the kitchen and had tea. Aunt Pedrina and Gramma were making sure everyone understood there was nothing to be afraid of. Gramma said this was very common in rural areas. When we finished the tea, the same happened with the conversation. Cousins Lucia and Pedro, the smallest ones, were already falling asleep. Gramma and Aunt Pedrina took them to bed. Because it was too late, Aunt Pedrina told us she would tell about the funeral the next morning. Thanks to the tea and the lateness of the hour, we all went to sleep.

The next morning, after breakfast and after we finished our chores in the orchard, we sat on the veranda to hear about the previous night's events. We were now fully awake and extremely interested in learning about the funeral. None of us had ever seen anything like that before. Being about a funeral in the middle of the night, with a body in the hammock, made what we were wishing to hear even more mysterious and interesting.

As promised, Aunt Pedrina was on the veranda to explain to us what had happened the night before. Everyone was quiet and attentive.

"I'm sorry this had to happen in the middle of the night; it made everything more frightening," she said. "Unfortunately, death does not make appointments; people die anytime and anywhere. We don't have to be old or sick to die, we just have to be alive. We should not be afraid of death. When we're born, no one knows if we're going to be smart, famous, or if we are going to have some special talent. We don't even know how long we're going to live. But we all know we are going to die one day or night. So we have to do the best we can all the time.

"Last night, the man they were taking to the next town to be buried died where he had lived all his life, in a small house in the woods next to the river. His friends and the family didn't have the necessary conditions to provide the dead with an appropriate burial. So they placed the body in a hammock to take it to the next town. They didn't have transportation. If they had had a vehicle, they would have put the body in the vehicle for the trip. Instead, they had to walk until they found someone who could help them. They carried candles, which they wrapped with white paper cones to protect the flame from the wind, but allow the light to pass through. Necessity is the mother of all inventions.

"As they walked, they chanted, 'for the soul, for the soul, for the soul.' That was what you heard," she said to me. "They were asking for help. In the darkness of the night, the candlelight helps others locate them. If people want to help, they put a light outside their houses. Their lights show permission for the travelers to come on to their property, and also, help the travelers locate them. Last night, Antonio offered to take them in his truck to the next town, which is not too far. Gramma and I gave them some money to help with the burial expenses."

All the kids were quiet, eager to hear what Aunt Pedrina had to say. "I have seen several funerals in the city, but nothing like last night," I said.

"Yes!" the rest of the kids replied in unison, in support of what I had just said.

"Well, last night's funeral was a situation created from poverty and isolation. However, different cultures and places have different preparations for burials. Some of the indigenous tribes bury their dead in special woven baskets with food and some personal belongings of the dead person. They believe that when someone dies, their soul has to go on a long journey to their final resting place. The food and the special things will make the journey more pleasant.

"The pharaohs of Egypt, in ancient time, had the same belief, but the ceremony was much more elaborate and costly. Their tombs are the famous pyramids that still exist today. They are considered one of the seven wonders of the world."

"I read in one of my school books that they used to mummify them before burial," said one of the kids, very proud of her knowledge.

"That's right. They developed a very sophisticated process to do that. In our culture, however, things are more simple; we place the body in the casket and bury it underground in the cemetery. We do put flowers and symbols, which represent the religious beliefs of the dead, over the grave after it has been covered with dirt. Unfortunately, as in the case of an Indian tribe and the pharaohs, in our culture, if the dead person is famous or very rich, the flowers, the symbols, and the casket are much more expensive. But if the dead person is very poor, you saw last night how they do it. In my opinion, we should have a burial ceremony very simple and equal for everyone."

That funeral had a long-lasting impression on me. I'll never forget those scary hours of darkness and the fear of what I didn't understand. Even today, after many years, when I look through the window of my apartment and I see the small city lights flickering in the distance, I remember the emotion of that night. Sometimes I can't help but think that someone may have died and I find myself saying, "May God bless their soul and give them eternal peace."

Thirteen
Saci Perere

The farm was a perfect setting for scary stories. It was dark around the houses, there were no outside lights, and because we were way out in the country, it was extremely quiet. If there were any noises, they would be small wild animals such as foxes, some kind of wild cat, groundhogs, or things flying around, like bats. Nine o'clock, after Antonio turned off the generator, it was a little spooky. Flickering oil lamps scattered around the farm created the right environment for mystery and suspense.

Many nights, Antonio or some of the other workers would come to the veranda after dinner to tell us some of their scary stories about ghosts and goblins. We would be scared to death. It was a terrifying experience that none of the kids would miss. We sat close to each other and as the narrative progressed, we would squeeze closer and closer. By the end of the story, if it had been a good one, we looked like a small bundle of arms and legs with several sets of big, nervous eyes.

They were folk tales. Aunt Pedrina told us they were not true. She said people liked to tell those stories just to scare the others. If they didn't scare anyone, they weren't fun. The success of a scary story was measured by the jumps and screams at the end. If everyone screamed and jumped, the story was a big success. That's why they liked to tell them to kids. Kids jump and scream at the end of a good scary story.

There were tales about big monsters and magic animals such as enormous snakes that could swallow a cow or a horse and horseman in one bite. Others were about magic horses that were able to fly in the night. Men and women without heads walking around, and countless others about strange beasts who lived beneath the surface of rivers and creeks. My favorite ones were about ghosts and haunted houses where supernatural creatures lived.

Aunt Pedrina knew how much we liked those spooky stories, so one day she promised us that after dinner she would tell us a folktale. It would not be too scary, but would be very interesting.

We brought some lamps to the veranda, not many because we wanted it to be a little dark and creepy to make the stories more believable and much more scary. We asked Olinda and Yolanda if they would like to go to the veranda after dinner. We told them Aunt Pedrina was going to tell us a folk tale. They both said no, they didn't like scary stories. They said they had trouble falling asleep after they got scared, and when they finally got to sleep, they had terrible nightmares.

All of the kids went to the veranda to hear Aunt Pedrina's tale. She came carrying her cloth bag; we used to call it her tricks bag. She always had something unexpected in it. We looked at each other with inquisitive glances, wondering what it was going to be about this time. We were afraid she would pull something from the bag that would make us jump. She sat down, placed the bag next to her seat, and started.

"People, especially children, like to believe in magic. Sometimes they create a special thing or a special belief to help them find an explanation for something they don't understand. Often, those images and special objects they believe in become part of folklore and are used in stories we call folk tales. The one I'm going to tell you tonight is about Saci Perere. It's a tale my grandmother told me long ago.

"Saci Perere is a baby devil from Brazilian mythology. He's a little boy who likes to play tricks on people who live in the country. He is not a creature of the city. He's very small and has only one leg, wears no clothing, just a red nightcap, and smokes a small terra cotta pipe. He's mischievous, but not dangerous.

"The fact that he has only one leg doesn't make it easy to hold him down. He travels inside a whirlwind that catches dry leaves and small twigs and spins them in the air. The leaves and twigs create a shield-like protection around him, making it difficult for people to see him. He likes to live in large, open fields, not too far from barns or any other places where farmers keep their horses. He prefers open fields because it's easy to move around in his whirlwind.

"Saci Perere likes to be near horses and fields because he loves horses and he loves riding them. If he can get hold of a horse, he will ride all night without stop. The next morning the farmer will find his horse exhausted, all sweaty, with its mane twisted into tiny, tight braids, impossible to undo. Saci braids the horse's mane when taking the ride.

"Farmers try to prevent Saci Perere from taking their horses by placing a figa outside the barn door or on the horses' necks. Figa is a wooden sculpture of a fist with all fingers closed, except the thumb, which points out between the index and the middle finger. Figa is originally from Africa and was introduced to our culture by the enslaved Africans. Many people believe that a figa can protect them from evil people or bad curses from witches, as well as keep Saci away from the horses. Another way to protect the horses is by having a necklace made of garlic hung outside the barn door. Garlic is a well-known protection against demons, witches, and other supernatural creatures, such as vampires. Another amulet that will keep Saci away from the horses is an old horseshoe with seven holes. That also should be hung on the barn door. One of those items, or a combination of the three, is believed to keep Saci Perere from harassing the horses.

"Traveling horsemen, when they stop to rest in the evening, use the same items in their horses' gear. They are afraid that while they are sleeping, their horse could be taken by Saci. The next morning the horse would be exhausted, incapable of continuing the journey.

"Some people try to catch Saci Perere. They believe if you catch Saci, it's the same as winning a big prize in the lottery, since he will give to his capturer anything in exchange for his freedom: fortune, knowledge, long life, treasures of gold and precious stones, a castle, lots of money, anything he or she wants. Although Saci is a very small creature, he is believed to have great power, and to be capable of turning into reality any dream of a mortal. He can only be caught with a small fishnet. The strategy is to throw the fishnet over the whirlwind, which will stop immediately, leaving the little devil tied to the ground unable to move, begging for his freedom. But you have to be very fast; whirlwinds move at a great velocity."

At that point of the narrative, which had captured our undivided attention, Aunt Pedrina reached for her cloth bag. All of the kids, with their eyes widely opened, in one synchronized motion, got in position to scream, jump, or run. Whatever would be necessary. We were afraid that Saci Perere would jump from her bag. Aunt Pedrina and Gramma, who was also sitting on the veranda, burst into a hearty laugh at us. They knew what was going on inside our heads.

"Calm down, calm down," she said. "Don't worry. If I had the little devil in my bag, I would not let him go free before he gave me everything I want. What I have here is a gift for you." She put her hand inside the bag and pulled several small fishnets from it. She gave one to each of us and told us to be prepared to catch Saci Perere and get everything we wanted.

We loved the story of the little devil, not just because it was an interesting tale, but especially because it gave us a chance for a great adventure; capture Saci and gain fame and fortune. We spent a long time, after that night, deciding what to ask for, in case one of us accomplished catching Saci Perere. We even went back to Aunt Pedrina to find out if we could only ask for one thing or if we could negotiate and get more than one thing, like lots of money and knowledge so we didn't have to go to school anymore. After all, we would have the upper hand. Walking in the field was never the same; we kept an eye out for whirlwinds. We never knew which one could bring us fortune, knowledge, or long life. One never knows.

Ghosts, goblins, magic monsters, and Saci Perere were not the only things we had to watch out for. We had to be aware of wild animals. The farm was surrounded with dense woods and the creek, which was the perfect habitat for all kinds of wild animals. They would come after dark and steal chickens, rabbits, baby goats, ducks, or any other small things. Every house on the farm had a dog that would bark furiously if it felt the presence of an unwelcome creature. Several times in the middle of the night, we heard shots to scare the wild animals and make them go back to the woods where they had come from.

I remember one late afternoon as dusk was approaching we were sitting and talking in the living room waiting for dinner, when Constancia came to the kitchen, by the back door, to bring some fresh eggs and some vegetables. Olinda was worried because it was getting dark.

"You should not be walking outside this time of the evening," she told Constancia. "Are you alone? Who came with you?" she asked, visibly upset.

"Only me and God," replied Constancia, casually.

"Only you two?" insisted Olinda.

Aunt Pedrina, who was listening to the conversation, smiled, and, shaking her head, went to the kitchen to rescue Constancia. "That's alright, Olinda. Don't worry about it. You're scaring everyone. Thanks for the eggs and vegetables, Constancia. That's very nice of you. The kids and I will walk you back home." Aunt Pedrina put her arm on Constancia's shoulder, who was a little embarrassed by Olinda's scene.

"Oh, Dona Pedrina, this is not necessary. I'm not afraid. I walk around here all the time," Constancia said, preparing to go.

"No, I insist. Besides, we don't want Olinda to have a heart attack." They all laughed. The kids were in the kitchen enjoying the little bit of melee.

Aunt Pedrina gave each of us a flashlight, except me. She gave me an empty can and a wood spoon. "O.K., we are ready to go now. Everyone, keep the flashlight on, and you (that was me), hit the wood spoon on that can as hard as you can and make lots of noise. The noise, the light, and, I'm sure, our giggles and chatter, will keep any wild thing far away from us."

Needless to say, we loved it. We felt like fearless warriors fighting dangerous wild animals to protect ladies in distress. As with everything we enjoyed on the farm, chasing wild animals became a new game we played often.

Aunt Pedrina, Gramma, everyone, including Antonio, told us repeatedly that the stories about ghosts, goblins, monsters, and Saci Perere were not real. They also told us the danger about wild animals had been grossly exaggerated. However, no one, not even Aunt Pedrina, had the power or the desire to limit our imagination. After all, everything was part of being a kid, growing up in an atmosphere full of culture and excitement. Those summers on Gramma's coffee farm would have a permanent place in our memories and one day we would tell them to our kids.

Fourteen
Treasure Hunting

Time was going by very fast, sometimes so fast we had to do a double-take in order to catch up with what was going on. Everyone was growing, some growing up, others growing older, but, nevertheless, growing. All the kids, now young adults, were becoming interested in different activities. We didn't spend much time as a group with Gramma and Aunt Pedrina anymore. We never stopped visiting them, but school vacation had become a different ball game. Some of us would spend it at the beach, others would participate in travel with our schools, going to faraway places where we would be exposed to new languages and cultures. Many of us had to take summer classes to repair the damages of the past school year.

Like everyone else, I was growing. Growing up, growing older, but I was also growing closer to Aunt Pedrina. Maybe because I was raised by my aunt and uncle, I was less attached to my home. Aunt Maria de Lurdes and Uncle Jose were extremely nice to me. I had the best money could buy, but was hungry for love and attention, which I found in abundance with Gramma and Aunt Pedrina. Aunt Pedrina and I were a perfect combination. She wanted a child and I needed a mother. I continued to spend part of my vacation with Gramma and her.

I loved to talk with her. She knew the most fascinating

stories. Every time I asked a question, whatever the subject may have been, she always had an answer and an interesting story to clarify the answer, except when I asked about the wildflowers she kept on her desk in the little crystal vase. When I asked where she had picked them up, she didn't give me a straight answer, as she always did for everything else. She smiled mischievously, glanced at the flowers and answered casually, "Everywhere . . . just . . . everywhere."

I remember one time when I came to stay with Gramma and Aunt Pedrina. It was late fall, the air was getting cold and we had lots of rain. Gramma told me that Aunt Pedrina was not feeling well; she had caught a bad cold. She gave me a container with hot chicken soup to take to her. "This soup, lots of juice, and rest, will get her well in no time," she said. I often heard, when chicken soup was on the stove, someone had been sick; either a member of the family or the chicken.

When I arrived at Aunt Pedrina's house, Olinda came to the door. She told me that Aunt Pedrina was in bed; she had been there all day reading. "I hope she'll have some of this soup, she's had nothing to eat all day," she said, going to the kitchen. I came in and closed the door behind me.

I heard Aunt Pedrina calling from her room, "Who's there, Olinda?" I guess she heard when I knocked on the door. I answered, telling her that it was just me. "Oh, what a nice surprise. Come upstairs," she replied, "I'd like to see you, but, please, cover your nose and mouth, I don't want you to catch my cold." We both chuckled and I walked into her room, defiant of any attacking cold germs.

When I got inside the room, she was seated against the headboard with several books in bed with her. I realized then that I had never, in all these years, seen her bedroom. It was a pleasant room located on the northeast corner of the house, a large room with four windows, two facing east and two facing north. The furniture was old, antique, I should say. Most of it appeared to be the consequence of many years of collecting, not what one would call a "set." Each piece was of different style and probably from different origin. However, they complemented each other and looked good together.

On the south side of the room, there was a large, solid, English style dresser made of jacaranda, a beautifully grained, dark, Brazilian hardwood, frequently used for fine furniture. Hanging on the wall above the dresser was a beautiful mirror with a carved wood frame. On the dresser was an enameled jewelry box and several pictures of the family, most of them in old, silver frames. Between the north windows was a small vanity that, like the rest of the furniture, was made of solid wood. The mirror, formed of three parts, could be moved to make it possible to see the back of the head of the person seated at the vanity. The frame of the mirror was also made of wood with elaborate hand carving. The stool for the vanity was stuffed and covered with antique gold velvet. In front of each of the windows on either side of the vanity was a comfortable chair. A large, oriental rug covered most of the floor. The bed was against the west wall. On the windows there were old drapes made of white lace. The room had a quiet, but undeniable dignity. I pulled one of the chairs close to the bed and we started to talk.

Olinda came with a bowl of soup and gave it to her. Aunt Pedrina was so involved in our conversation, asking questions about school, my life in the city, the family and such, that she finished the soup without knowing. We hadn't seen each other for a few months. As we continued to talk, I told her it was the first time I had seen her bedroom.

"Aunt Pedrina, your room is very nice. I like all of your

furniture, but I'm intrigued by your bed. It's the most unusual piece of furniture you have. I've never seen anything like it."

"Oh, it's just an old lady's room full of old things, old ideas, and old memories, but you're right, my bed is unique and so is the story of how I got it. Would you like to hear it?"

"Sure! I'd love to."

"When I first got married I had an empty house and a head full of ideas. I didn't want to go to a furniture store and buy a bunch of new furniture. I like to find things that are different and in good taste. I'm like you, I have loved antiques since I was very young, but Luiz and I were just starting out and we had a small budget, so I had to go around looking for bargains. In the beginning, it was a necessity, but I enjoyed my treasure hunting so much I continued to do it all my life. I often found interesting and beautiful things for the house, like my little writing desk downstairs. But this bed I'm very proud of. I designed it myself using an old part of another piece. This was many years after Luiz passed away."

I stood up to take a closer look at the headboard. "It's really beautiful. Where did you find it?"

"One day, after I had retired from teaching at Indian Creek, I decided to paddle my canoe once more and go visit the schoolhouse and some friends. I missed being around the students, the school, and some of the farmers with whom I had become friends. All of them had continued living on the other side of the river. I called Olinda and told her we were going to Indian Creek. She was a little surprised that I had said 'we.' Well, I think surprised understates her reaction.

"I'm sorry, Dona Pedrina! I'm afraid of water. I don't know how to swim, I don't think 'we' are going anywhere because I'm not going in that canoe. I'm scared. I'm too scared and I'm not going,' she said and rushed back to the kitchen. I wasn't going to give up that easily, so I followed her.

"I said, 'Come on, Olinda. Do you think I would do anything dangerous? Anything that would put you at risk? Don't worry, it's going to be fun. You'll love it, besides, it's just a fifteen minute ride. You have nothing to be scared of.' It wasn't easy, but I convinced her to go along after I promised that Juca, not I, would paddle the canoe back and forth.

"When we got into the canoe, Olinda sat down stiff like a board, holding a little umbrella like it was her security blanket, scared to death. For the entire fifteen minutes of the ride, I think she didn't breathe, afraid to turn the canoe upside down. When we arrived on the other side, Juca helped her out of the canoe. I stared at her, inquisitively, without saying anything.

" 'O.K., O.K.,' she said, guessing what I wanted to know. 'It was not too bad. In fact, I believe I would have enjoyed it if I hadn't been so scared.' I told her I had told her so, we giggled about it, and then walked together toward the schoolhouse. Juca stayed on the riverbank to do some fishing.

"Olinda was impressed with the building and the surroundings. The schoolhouse was small and quaint, but looked loved. The front yard had some good-looking plants and a well-kept lawn with two unusual flowering trees, I don't know what they were, planted on each side of the front steps. The students and their parents volunteered for the yard work. When they rebuilt the school long ago, I suggested to them to build a teachers' quarters so we could have one or two teachers living there during the school year. After visiting the school and talking with the new teachers for a while, I borrowed the school car and went with Olinda to visit some of my friends.

"When we got to Jacinto's farm, Jacinto and his wife, Anita, were pleased to see us. Anita was a dear friend. When I was teaching in Indian Creek, she often used to come see me after classes. She was happy that I still counted them as friends and had not forgotten them. After we talked for a while and I was getting ready to leave, Anita told me that the string beans and the zucchinis were very good that year and she wanted me and Olinda to go with her to pick some.

"As we walked towards the vegetable garden, we passed by the pig pen, and it was there that I saw it. The fence of the pen was made of different pieces of wood. Old doors, parts of old windows, building materials, or any thing that would help to keep the pigs where they belonged, in the pig pen. One of these pieces appeared to be the back of an old wooden bench. It was filthy, covered with mud and several layers of paint of different colors. When I told them I would like to buy that piece of wood, they laughed. They couldn't believe I wanted that piece of garbage. Olinda joined them laughing at me.

"I explained I like old things and I was going to try to do something with that 'piece of garbage.' I finally convinced Jacinto to take some money to buy wood to fill the hole in the fence. Reluctantly, he accepted the money and offered to bring 'that thing' in his truck to my house.

"At that time, there was an elderly gentleman in town, Mr. Marcolino, who was quite talented and did beautiful work restoring and refinishing antiques. I knew him well since he had already done some work for me. After Jacinto delivered my valuable discovery, I called Mr. Marcolino to estimate the cost of stripping and refinishing the bench back. When he saw what I had bought, he also laughed at me. ‘Dona Pedrina, you’re wasting your money on that one,’ he said. ‘I think you should throw this thing out. It isn’t good and smells really bad.’

“‘Never mind about the smell,’ I told him. ‘Olinda and I will wash it clean and get rid of the smell. As far as the value of this piece, it’s too early to come to any conclusion. Just tell me the cost of your work. That’s all I’m interested in,’ I told him. I was kind of annoyed, but so many people laughing at me had made me even more determined to see this through to completion.

“After we argued back and forth about the price, we finally came to an agreement. I told him to give me a week to clean it and let it dry, then he could come get it. When he left, he was still scoffing and shaking his head. A week went by and he came back. I believe he was sorry for having laughed at me. This time he was quiet, more businesslike. After all, I was a good customer. I told him to strip all the paint and sand it, but not to refinish it until I had a chance to see the natural wood so I could decide what to do with it. About two weeks later, he sent someone to tell me that he would like to see me at his workshop.

“When I got there, Mr. Marcolino held himself with an air of quiet authority. I could see in his eyes that he, the expert, had warned me of my foolishness. The bench back was half-stripped. On the top corner of both sides, it had some kind of metal showing. He asked me, ‘Dona Pedrina, this is no good. It’s full of nails, and it’s probably all broken. Do you want me to continue?’ I looked very carefully at what he said were nails. ‘Do you know something, Mr. Marcolino? I don’t believe these are nails. First of all, they are too shiny, and second, they have a curve that appears to be the same on both sides. Do me a favor, strip around ‘those nails’ a bit more. I want to see more of them.’

“After a little work, we were able to better see the

metal, and he looked surprised and a little excited. 'Dona Pedrina, you're right, these aren't nails. This is an inlay of silver wire. It's an interesting design and is really beautiful.' Well . . . Guess who had now one of those 'I told you so' looks. He completed stripping and sanding the bench back, which, it turned out, was made of mahogany. The final product was stunning, We could see the magnificent silver incrustation and the beauty of the design. The finished piece looked so good that I decided to use it to make the headboard of my bed."

"Whaw! That is really neat. Did you know it was what it was?" I asked.

"No, I did not. What caught my attention was the shape of the cut. I had no idea what to do with it. But, in life, we must take some risks. We just have to make sure there's no chance of it becoming a catastrophic risk. Besides, always, the most precious things in life are the ones we discover. All the beauty of this world would be wasted if we did not stop to discover and admire it."

Aunt Pedrina knew how much I liked her bed and her desk, the small one with the little crystal vase on top always full of wildflowers. She left both for me in her will. Until today, they are my most valued possessions.

Fifteen
The Engagement Ring

Mirante was also growing and wasn't so little anymore. I made lots of new friends there. Many of the young people who had left town to go to different schools would come back home for summer vacation. We had countless activities to pass the time: fishing, boating on the river (yes, I learned how to paddle a canoe), long horseback rides, picnics with lots of good food, and lots of games. And, of course, parties, the best ones, full of music, dancing, and camaraderie.

Gramma and Aunt Pedrina made me feel welcome every time I visited and tried their best to make sure I had a good time. Gramma also welcomed my friends to spend some time at the farm, which was one of the best parts of our vacation.

Aunt Pedrina had a 1940 Oldsmobile, in very good shape. It looked like new. She didn't drive much. The car was in the garage most of the time. Mauro, the best mechanic in town, took good care of the engine; it worked like a Swiss clock. Juca and I were in charge of washing and polishing. She knew I loved to drive, so she invented chores for me that required some driving. Even though years had passed, she hadn't changed, she was still so thoughtful and enjoyable to be around.

She was just a regular person. She didn't sit at her little

desk waiting for someone to come by so she could teach them the golden rules. She did everything like you and I. For instance, she loved to watch a good soccer game on television. We did watch many games together. She didn't just watch the game; she participated. She would become really involved. Often, she was so mad with some player or the referee that they were lucky she couldn't reach them.

After dinner, with Olinda, she liked to sit down to watch television and sip on a good Portuguese port wine. She also liked to smoke a cigarette occasionally. When we were kids, we used to laugh and say that her house didn't have mosquitoes because she killed them with the smoke from her cigarettes. They were strong ones.

When I came for vacation, I did my best to help out. The yard was still her favorite hobby. She loved her plants. Juca was getting old, he was almost Aunt Pedrina's age, around eighty, and he didn't work for anyone anymore, just now and then for Aunt Pedrina, although he could only do small jobs. So she left all the big projects for the summer when I was there. I liked to work in the yard because it usually included one or two trips to the Commercial Center to buy plants, fertilizer or other things for the garden. That required some driving, of course.

One summer she told me she would like to redo one of the flowerbeds in the front yard. New plants, maybe a small garden cement statue, and a small flowering tree on the left side, which was the sunny side of the yard. First, I had to dig up the old plants carefully because some of them would be replanted. After that, I had to loosen up the soil, remove all the weeds, add fertilizer, and prepare it for the new and the re-planting of the old plants. Juca was there to oversee the work and teach me how to do it right.

Aunt Pedrina liked to sit on a stool and watch me work. She loved working in the garden, and would have been doing the digging herself, but could no longer do it. She was limited to watching and giving opinions. After I removed the old plants and the weeds, I grabbed the pick and started to dig. When I pulled up the second chunk of dirt, I heard a scream that made me freeze. I turned around to see what was going on. Aunt Pedrina was standing up screaming, "My ring, my ring, my engagement ring!" Juca and I stared at her trying to understand why she was screaming. She was hysterical. She was pointing to the chunk of dirt, frantically yelling, "My ring, get my ring. Oh my goodness, I can't believe it, my engagement ring!"

I looked in the direction she was pointing and there, in the overturned soil, was a shiny circle. It was a small ring made of a gold-colored metal with two stones, a red one and another I didn't recognize, covered with dirt. I reached down into the dirt, shook the ring and gave it to her. She held it tight in her hand and for the first time in my life, I saw her cry. It was a happy cry because at the same time her teary eyes were shut tight, she smiled blissfully.

She opened her hand and stared in disbelief. Carefully, she removed the dirt like she was caressing a loved one. She looked at Juca and me with amazement, a mixture of shock and happiness. Still crying and smiling, she said in a soft voice, almost whispering, "This is my engagement ring. Luiz gave it to me when we became engaged." She stared at her cupped palm for a long, silent moment, remembering long-faded joy. Then, some memory caused her to look up from her hand. She saw Juca and me before her and was once again aware of the present. To let us know she was back with us again in the yard, working in the garden, she began to tell us about the ring. "This style was very popular when I was young. They called it Romeo and Juliet. It's made of gold and, see here, together, it has a ruby and a pearl. It was specially designed for engagements.

Girls were so proud of wearing one because it meant someone loved you and wanted to marry you. My heavens, I can't believe this. It was lost for more than sixty years. The pearl is badly damaged, but the rest is in perfect condition. I'm so happy."

"How did you lose it? It must have been really upsetting for you," I asked curiously.

"When we first got married, Uncle Luiz kept a horse he had had since he was a boy. He built a small barn in the backyard for it. During the day, the horse stayed behind our house, where, at that time, there was an open pasture. In the evening, Luiz brought him to his stall. His name was Big Boy. He was a small horse, almost the size of a pony.

"One afternoon I was helping Luiz feed Big Boy. I was loosening a section of a bale of alfalfa to give to him, and, I believe in doing so, I pulled my ring off. I didn't notice until we went back to the house and I started to wash my hands. Luiz, Olinda, and I turned the barn upside down. We looked for this ring everywhere for months. We never found it. I never made the connection before, but every time Luiz removed the straw bedding in the barn to put a new one, he used the old bedding to make compost for fertilizing the garden. That's how, I think, the ring ended up buried in the flower bed.

"Anyway, I continued to cry and look for my ring for a long, long time. Uncle Luiz wanted to give me another one just like it. I told him I didn't want another one. It was a special ring; it couldn't be replaced."

Olinda came running from the house; she had heard Aunt Pedrina screaming. When she got to where we were, she saw the ring and heard Aunt Pedrina telling the story of how she had lost her engagement ring.

"Oh! I remember that night," she said smiling. "Nobody slept in this house or in the barn that night, not even

Big Boy. We all spent the night in his barn looking for the ring, everywhere. The next day we walked from the house to the barn, back and forth a thousand times. We looked, so carefully, over every inch of the ground. We cleaned the barn, took everything out, and we shook everything little by little, very carefully, trying to find this ring. I can't believe you found it." She looked to Aunt Pedrina and said, "You scared me to death. You're still capable of a pretty good scream, you know? When I heard your scream, I thought something terrible had happened. Thank God, it's something good."

"I'm sorry. I didn't mean to scare anyone, but when I saw the ring, I thought I was going to explode. I couldn't believe it myself. After all these years, I have my ring back."

"Let's continue to dig," Juca said enthusiastically. "Maybe we'll find some more gold." Together, the four of us laughed. We were delighted by Aunt Pedrina's happiness.

"Aunt Pedrina, what happened to Big Boy?" I asked.

"After Uncle Luiz died, your Grampa took him to the farm. He was getting old and the farm had more room for grazing and more people to take care of him. We demolished the barn and in its place we planted the eucalyptus tree.

"I think finding my ring calls for a celebration. Olinda, let's give a cold glass of iced tea to our gold diggers." We walked together to the kitchen and gave ourselves the rest of the afternoon to be carried along in the current of Aunt Pedrina's memories of her young husband.

Sixteen
The Dinner Guest

For the time I passed in the company of Gramma and Aunt Pedrina, there were always some fun and interesting things planned for me. But I don't think I was the only one who benefited from my visit. I like to believe they enjoyed my company and appreciated my help with some of the work around the house. Of all the projects, the ones I liked best were taking them shopping, going to see a movie, or visiting some of their friends. I would be the designated driver. After I dropped them off, I'd go for a ride, a long one, then come back to pick them up.

Driving the old Oldsmobile was my favorite job. It made me feel important. When I drove around, I probably looked pretty silly, a permanent smile stretched across my face as if the skin around my lips had shrunk and I couldn't close my mouth. Besides my help, I like to believe they enjoyed my company and my stories about the rest of the family. I was their link between the capital and the little town.

I remember one time I was there for a long weekend. Uncle Jose had some papers for Gramma to sign and have notarized. He took care of the legal and financial affairs of both Aunt Pedrina and Gramma.

When I got there, Aunt Pedrina told me that we had been invited to dinner by a good friend of hers, Mrs. Margarida Oliveira. She told me this lady knew me when I was little and had not seen me for long time. Aunt Pedrina said they were talking one day and my name came up in the conversation. She told the lady that I was growing; I was in my late teens and was doing well in school and had turned into a pleasant young man. The lady said she would like to see me. She had not seen me for more than ten years. When Aunt Pedrina told her I was coming for the weekend, she invited us for dinner.

Aunt Pedrina told me she was a close friend of hers whom she had known since they were young girls. They used to go together to parties and church functions. Meg, as Margarida was called, was married to Rogerio Oliveira, who was also a longtime friend. He had been friends with Uncle Luiz since childhood. They used to go on double dates when they were teenagers. I thought this was going to be fun. I probably would hear some old stories about places and people I didn't know. I always liked to hear stories from the good old days.

Aunt Pedrina told me to take the car (oh, boy!) and go to the flower shop in town and buy a beautiful bouquet of flowers for me to take to Mrs. Oliveira. She said it was the proper thing to do. I was kind of embarrassed to go to the dinner carrying flowers. I asked Aunt Pedrina if she would be the one who carried the flowers and she said no, this was the gentleman's job. It is proper for a gentleman to give flowers to the lady of the house when invited for dinner. I believed her, but felt uncomfortable for being a gentleman. I hoped none of my friends would see me with the flowers.

Before I left, I asked if there was anything more she wanted me to do. She smiled and said, "No, you will have a chance to drive a little more when we go for dinner." *She could read me like a book*, I thought.

I changed my shirt and combed my hair. I wanted to make a good impression driving that beauty. From behind the steering wheel to the front chrome grill seemed half of a soccer field. The hood ornament soared out before me like the figurehead on the prow of a clipper ship. When I got to town, before I headed to the flower shop, I drove two or three times around the main square to see if some of my friends were there, but, most of all, just to be seen driving the car. Today, no one important was around so I headed to the flower shop.

The florist was located in a small shopping center along with several other shops specializing in items for the house, like a hardware, a stationery and card store, and a sewing and craft store. When I was approaching the flower shop, I saw a parking space right in front of the store. I headed for it when some woman came from nowhere and cut me off, almost smashing into the front fender, and parked in the same spot. Boy, I got angry. I jumped out and cursed her. I called her an irresponsible idiot, a stupid fool who should not be allowed to drive a car. I was not angry just for losing the parking spot; there were many others. I was shaken up by her near collision with Aunt Pedrina's beautiful car that, fortunately, had good brakes. If it hadn't, we would have had a nasty crash.

The woman didn't say anything. She put her head down and almost ran into the sewing shop. I got in the car, backed up, and parked in another spot. I stayed in the car for a few minutes, until I had a chance to cool off before I went to the flower shop. I bought the flowers and went right back home. I drove exceedingly cautiously; no big smile and no casual pose. The incident had spoiled my day. I didn't say anything to Aunt Pedrina; I was afraid she would lose the confidence she had in my driving.

I spent the rest of the day working in both Gramma and Aunt Pedrina's front yards. I wanted to keep busy to take my mind off the narrowly-avoided catastrophe in the shopping center. Another thing that was bothering me was to decide if I should or should not tell Aunt Pedrina about what happened. At the end of the day, I was feeling better and my knees had stopped shaking, and I had decided the stress of the near-accident was mine to bear and there was no reason to burden anyone else with the unpleasantness. I took a shower and got dressed for the dinner. Aunt Pedrina told me I had to wear a jacket and tie. I felt foolishly formal, all dressed up carrying a bouquet of flowers.

The Oliveira's house was not too far, just in the outskirts of town in a well-manicured neighborhood of beautiful homes. Aunt Pedrina pointed out to me which one was Meg's house. It was a large, traditional brick house with an imposing entrance surrounded by a well-kept garden. The front yard, like the whole house, had lots of space. On the right side was an area reserved for parking. I parked the car, opened the door for Aunt Pedrina, and together; she, the flowers and I, walked to the front door.

I had the impression the bouquet had become bigger, more colorful, and more difficult to carry; I couldn't decide which way was the proper way to hold it. I expected a maid would come to open the door after we rang the bell, but instead, Mrs. Oliveira herself came to greet us. I had the shock of my life. I felt like I was shrinking and the bouquet was growing. The air became heavy. I couldn't breathe, my pulse was one hundred miles an hour. I wished I could dig a big hole in the ground and bury myself. Meg, the good friend, the lady of that magnificent house, the one who wished to see me and had invited me for dinner was, no more, no less than the same woman I had insulted that morning in the shopping center! The same one I had called irresponsible and stupid!

The only thing I wanted to do was throw those flowers in the air and run. Run as fast as I could to the farthest possible place. To Aunt Pedrina's house, back to the capital, to the moon, maybe. My luck was that I could not move either my arms or my legs. I was paralyzed, like rusted armor, and held up the bouquet of flowers as a barricade behind which I was hiding my bright red face.

Margarida casually smiled and addressed Aunt Pedrina, "Good evening, Pedrina. How nice to see you again. This must be your grandnephew about whom you spoke so very highly." She said without facing me, "Please come in."

We followed her to what appeared to be a sitting room. I sat in one of the chairs, upright and stiff, holding those silly flowers in front of me like a shield. Aunt Pedrina sat and addressed her friend. "Meg, those flowers are for you. Maybe they should be placed in water."

The maid brought a tray of hors d'oeurves and took the flowers away. I felt naked and exposed. Mr. Oliveira joined us in the sitting room. "Pedrina, how nice see you again. This must be your grandnephew whom we haven't seen for a long time. I wouldn't recognize him if I saw him in any other place." He kissed Aunt Pedrina on the cheek and shook hands with me. He gave Meg and Aunt Pedrina a glass of sherry wine, himself a scotch, and a soda for me. I guess I was old enough to insult people, but not old enough to have a drink with them.

My luck was that the conversation was more about themselves. Thank God. Of course, he asked me about school, what I was taking and my plans for the future, all the regular things an adult asks a kid, without being really interested in the answer. I had never felt more uncomfortable and more out of place. Each ticking second of their casual conversation, I was praying the dinner would not last too long. After forever, the maid came to announce that dinner was served. I breathed. I stood. We passed through to the dining room.

The dinning room was elegant and traditional, the table covered with white linen, and beautifully arranged with fine crystal, china, and exclusive silverware. After Meg indicated our seats, we sat and they continued their conversation. They seemed to be fond of each other and happy for being together. I was glad I wasn't the center of attention, I was being politely ignored. But my good luck was coming to an end.

For no reason, Aunt Pedrina started to brag about me, how nice and considerate I was, a perfect gentleman. I could feel Meg's look burning my face. I didn't dare face her. I knew she knew what Aunt Pedrina was saying was not entirely the truth. She had had the opportunity to witness the reality of my gentlemanly qualities. She had met the real me and learned firsthand how much of the gentleman I really was.

Dinner was finally over, again, thank God. To me, it felt like it had lasted an eternity. Following the usual good-byes and promises to see each other again soon, we left. I was silent and still, exhausted by the enormous tension. Aunt Pedrina was watching me, puzzled. I knew I was in serious trouble. After a brief silence she said, "What's wrong with you? You are extremely quiet. I don't recall you ever being so tongue-tied like this before. Didn't you like Meg and Rogerio or didn't you like the food? You didn't say anything or eat much of anything. What's the matter?"

I knew I could no longer hide the truth. It was time for me to take responsibility for what I had done. It was going to be difficult, but in some way I welcomed the chance to put an end to this unbearable state of affairs. I told her what had happened that morning at the shopping center. I told the story with all the glorious details.

Aunt Pedrina was quiet for a few seconds. Finally, without looking at me, she said, "Well, I'm surprised by your behavior. Undoubtedly, it's a side of your personality I had no idea existed. It's difficult for me to believe you could be so rude to anyone, much less to a lady. I'm shocked."

"But, Aunt Pedrina," I responded defensively, "she almost wrecked your car. I think what she did was very rude, too." I was bruised by her reaction and clung tightly to the steering wheel for support.

"I understand, but just think. The fact that someone did something you consider rude does not justify your own rudeness. You'll be doing the same thing to the other person that you thought was wrong. Two wrongs do not equal one right. When you're angry, upset, and out of control, you should never say or do anything. The best thing is to walk away from the situation and give your temper a chance to cool, then react.

"My mother taught me something I never forgot. Before you say anything to anyone, when you're angry, you should ask yourself three questions: 'Is it true?' 'Is it kind?' And, 'Is it necessary?' If the answer for any of these questions is 'no,' don't say it. If you do, you'll regret it later.

"Meg is not a rude person. I've known her all my life. She probably didn't see you. Meg can be dreadfully vain; she needs glasses badly, but she refuses to wear them. She probably was as upset and angry with herself as you were. She also, probably, was embarrassed for what she did. But you can be sure she is not a rude, mean, or thoughtless person. She's kind and polite, incapable of purposely offending anyone."

I was even more miserable and angry with myself. "I guess now is too late for the three questions, and your mother was right, I do regret what I said. But what can I do to undo what I did?"

"Well, in my opinion, tomorrow you should go back to the flower shop and buy another bouquet of flowers, much larger than the first one, go back to Meg's house to apologize and thank her for not embarrassing you by telling everyone about the encounter she had with you in the shopping center. Tell her what you just told me about your concern for my car and how sorry you are for being so rude. She'll understand and most likely will apologize to you as well."

"Are you going with me?" I begged.

"Oh no. In life, sometimes, we have to go places we would rather not. But, we can't help it. We must go, and must go alone."

So much for my first fancy dinner party, I thought. "Do you think I should call before I go?" I asked. I didn't want to take any chances. I wanted to do everything just right this time.

"I don't think so," she answered. "Usually, the right thing is to call before you go to someone's house. But, in this situation, I think getting her by surprise would be more agreeable."

I did exactly what Aunt Pedrina told me to do. She was right. Mrs. Oliveira was pleasant and understood everything. She told me not to worry about it, this would be our secret. She did apologize to me and said she was sorry for almost causing an accident, but she didn't mention anything about needing glasses. She gave me a kiss on the cheek and said, "Pedrina is right, you are a nice young man."

I went back home feeling a little better. I was driving slowly, trying to remember the three questions. "How does that go, I can't remember . . . Oh yes. 'Is it true?' 'Is it kind?' and 'Is it necessary?' Oh boy, I do have a lot to learn."

Seventeen
Good Friends

Mrs. Oliveira and I became, eventually, good friends. It was difficult in the beginning for me to relax around her. The memory of that dreadful day at the shopping center was still pretty much alive in my mind. The more I got to know her, the more I disliked what I had done. She was a neat lady, extremely polite, kind, and understanding. She was just as Aunt Pedrina had described her.

Aunt Pedrina knew how I felt about the whole situation and tried to talk to me about it, but I avoided the subject. One afternoon, I came back from the local library where I had spent most of the day studying. Olinda came to tell me that Aunt Pedrina wished to see me. I set my books down, grabbed a piece of cake, and was on my way.

When I entered Aunt Pedrina's study, she appeared to be in a very good mood. She asked me how I was doing, how was my day at the library. She told me that when she was young she spent a lot of time at the same library. But I knew her well; all that preliminary small talk was a sign that something important was coming. Finally, she asked me to sit down and told me she wanted to talk with me.

"I want you to listen to everything I have to say with attention," she said calmly. "We will proceed according to a rule that we'll establish; I'll talk and you listen without interruption. When I finish, you talk and I'll listen, no interruption. Agree?" She didn't seem to be upset. In fact, she was cordial and relaxed.

"Agreed," I answered. "I'll listen to everything you have to say, but whether I'll have anything to say afterwards, I don't know. I have no idea what you want to talk about. Let's hear it." I looked at her and tried to guess the reason for the impending discussion.

"I know you're still uncomfortable facing Meg and you've been avoiding her company. I also know how sorry you are because you learned you can be rude with a person who made you angry. You're probably more disturbed by discovering your ability to be so unpleasant than Meg is for having been the focus of your anger. She's an intelligent woman who raised three children and isn't easily surprised. She's well aware of how, sometimes, things can get out of hand. She accepted your apology and felt equally responsible for what happened. She also knows that for every problem there is a solution. So please, stop feeling guilty and look at what happened as a valuable learning experience.

"As far as the possibility of you becoming rude again in a stressful situation, you have to develop the skill to control yourself. There is so much about ourselves we don't know. We can predict how we would like to react in different situations. However, the truth of the matter is, we aren't sure. We have no way of knowing what our reaction will be until we actually face the situation. The more we expose ourselves to difficult conditions, the more we become aware of our potential for heroic or evil behavior. And, of course, the more we know our weaknesses, the better chance we have to become strong and control ourselves.

"As a result of this disagreeable incident, you learned that given the right circumstances, you can be very unpleasant. In the future, if you find yourself in a similar situation, you have to force yourself to walk away and avoid the malice. And this will be a heroic decision. What do you think?"

"Whaw! What a speech. Have you ever considered running for public office?" I asked.

"Yes, once. I wanted to be the president, but you kids kept me too busy." We both looked at each other and smiled silently for a moment, and then started to talk about something different. She knew I wasn't ready yet to discuss the subject objectively.

Everything she said made a lot of sense. That conversation was helpful. I was able to, gradually, overcome my guilt and began to accept the whole thing, like she said, as a learning experience.

Meg was not the only one of the many friends of Aunt Pedrina that I met and became close to. Everyone had some special qualities. She chose her friends the same way she chose her plants; they had to be unique and exceptional. I always enjoyed meeting them and in many cases became close friends with them. One of her friends who impressed me a great deal was Airton da Silva, a former student of hers.

Airton da Silva was a lawyer who kept one office there in the little town and another in the capital where he lived with his wife and children. The only reason he kept an office in Mirante was to be able to give something back to the place that had made it possible for him to become what he was. He represented for free anyone who could not afford a lawyer. He was a good friend of Aunt Pedrina's and always referred to her as Aunt Pedrina. I know a lot about him because he told me.

One day, Aunt Pedrina gave me an envelope to take to him at his office. When I got there, he shook my hand and smiled broadly, like he was pleased to see me. "So, you are the grandnephew she talks about all the time, the one she is so proud of. She told me you are doing remarkably well in school. Nice to meet you. Please have a seat."

"Thanks, but I don't want to take much of your time. Aunt Pedrina told me that you usually don't stay in town too long and how busy you are," I answered, continuing to stand.

"I'm never too busy for Aunt Pedrina or anyone of her family. Without her, I would have nothing to do besides deliver bread. Did she ever tell you how we met?"

"I don't think so," I said. "I know she knows you well and she is proud of you, but that's all I know."

"Good, would you like to know?" he asked. "It's a good story and one that I'm happy to tell. It's about how love and kindness changed my life. Please, have a seat."

"Sure, I'd like to hear it, if you have time," I said. I was a bit uncomfortable because I was afraid I was taking him away from his legal work. But he seemed at ease, and I was interested to hear the story, so I settled into a chair next to his desk.

"When my family moved to this town," he started, "I was about thirteen. I was born and raised on a small farm about seventy miles from here. I lived there with my mother, father, a brother, and a sister. My father worked for the farmer who owned the land and I worked with my father. I didn't have a chance to go to school: there was no school around and my family was too poor to send me away to school. Besides, I was the oldest of the children. My father needed my help. He wasn't well and couldn't do all of the work by himself.

"When my father died, we had to move because the farmer needed our house for another worker and his family. My mother decided to move to town. She needed a job to support the family that had become totally dependent on her. The only job she was qualified for was working as a maid, and in town, she would have a better chance to find employment.

"She found a job and a small place for us to live. I was excited because, in town, I thought, maybe, I would have the opportunity to go to school. But it wasn't possible. I had to help my mother because she was unable to support the family by herself. The life in the city is easier, but also more expensive. I got a job as a delivery boy at the bakery.

"Part of my job was to deliver bread to the cafeteria at the local high school. I used to stop and lean on the fence of the recreation area and watch the kids. I used to dream I was also a student. Every day I would walk around and if I found an empty classroom, I would sit down and pretend I was taking a class. I imagined the teacher and my classmates all there with me. It was my biggest fantasy. Frequently, it was hard to go back to reality. I'd walk away carrying the bread basket as if it were my bookbag.

"Another place I had to deliver bread was Aunt Pedrina's house. I knew she was a teacher who had helped lots of kids in town. I was getting too old to go to grammar school and I wanted to meet her and ask for her help. Every time I went there, it was Olinda who answered the door. I always tried to look over her shoulder to try to see the teacher. One day, Olinda looked at me, kind of annoyed, and said, 'What's the matter with you, young man? Every time you deliver bread, you keep looking over my shoulder. What are you looking for?'

"I was embarrassed, but I told her I was trying to see the teacher. She said 'Why didn't you say so? Do you want to talk with Dona Pedrina?' She was less annoyed. I didn't know what to say, but I guessed it was too late to back out and ended up saying yes. So, she told me, 'O.K., you stay here; I'll call her,' and went into the house. Oh, boy, I was nervous and almost sorry I had said something. When she came back, Aunt Pedrina was with her. She was friendly. She could tell I was nervous and embarrassed. She smiled and greeted me, 'Good morning. Olinda tells me you wanted to talk with me. What can I do for you?' She noticed I was uncomfortable so she tried to make it easy for me, 'What's your name? You're new in town, aren't you? Don't be nervous, it can't be that bad. Whatever it is, you can tell me. If you don't tell me, there's nothing I can do to help you. Go on, what's the matter?'

"I felt she was sincere and she really wanted to hear what I had to say. I started out kind of mumbling. I said my name, but had to repeat it twice. I think I was pronouncing all the words like it was one big syllable. As I continued to talk, I spoke louder and more slowly. Gradually, I became more understandable. She listened attentively, nodding her head and gesturing to encourage me to continue to tell my story. She told me, 'You see, that wasn't so bad. Come in and have a seat and tell me exactly what you would like to do.'

"I was more comfortable now. Her friendliness and kindness were a great incentive. Olinda was standing up against the entrance of what appeared to be a living room. I told her I hadn't been to school, ever, and how much I wanted to learn how to read and write. I also told her that I knew I was too old for grammar school, which I could not go to anyway because I had to work. I explained how I needed to help my mother and why we had moved to the city.

"She listened carefully. Olinda, her eyebrows sympathetic, her eyes knowing, was listening with compassionate curiosity. My story was, probably, similar to her own. Aunt Pedrina looked at me inquisitively and declared, 'I don't think it would be too difficult for you to learn how to read and write. And, what do you intend to do after you learn that?' She had this probing look, like she was trying to read my thoughts. I told her about my dream to go to high school. 'They have night classes, you know?' I said. She smiled approvingly, just like Olinda. They were pleased with my answer, 'I don't foresee any reason why we couldn't do that, if it's really what you want. I will help you, but before we start, we have to talk with your mother. She has to approve our plans. When can we talk with her?' She was ready to take action.

"I made all the arrangements and she met my mother, who was pleased to know her and enthusiastic about our plans. My mother was grateful to Aunt Pedrina for wanting to help us. Every afternoon after work I went to her house. I started to learn immediately. I was like a dry sponge, eagerly absorbing every explanation. Slowly, I memorized the alphabet, learned syllable sounds, and then started to read everything Aunt Pedrina gave me. It was overwhelming to be able to understand all those symbols and transform them into sounds that were words with meaning, words that represented not only ideas, but also emotions, fears, and desires as well. In a short time I was able to draw the symbols that represented my own thoughts. I had learned how to write. At the same time I was learning mathematics, science, geography, and history. History was my favorite subject, probably because of the way she taught it; she had an uncanny ability to tell stories. She talked about things that happened a long time ago like she was there when it happened. She made sure I understood what happened, when, where, why, and who was involved. And when she talked about who was involved, she would tell you everything about them. They would come to life. Whatever places or people she spoke of, I felt like I had been there also, and knew all of them well.

"After one year's time and a great deal of work, she made the arrangements for me to take the examination to enter into high school. Everyone in the school system knew she was preparing me for it. I passed with flying colors and was admitted to the high school. I was so proud, I skipped around town beaming like a lighthouse. I told everyone who was interested and everyone who wasn't. My mother and I cried and hugged until we were exhausted. I was a high school student. Do you know what that meant? I'm sorry, of course you know, you are one. But for me, my fantasy had become reality. Later, I used to go to the recreation area and look over the fence to see if I could see that boy with a bread basket and a dreamer's gaze. But he was no longer there. He had grown, learned, and transformed his dream into reality.

"She continued to work with me diligently and made sure I wouldn't have any problems. I finished high school with a 4.0 average. When I was a senior, she was already working with her friends in the capital to get me a scholarship to the national university. She organized a group of her friends in town to sponsor me because, although I didn't have to pay tuition, I needed money for room and board, books, clothes, etc. I did work part-time, but the money I earned was not enough for all of my expenses. It was like the whole town had adopted me.

"I took preparatory courses and then applied to the law school. I continued to do well. I took all my classes very seriously. After my first year in law school, I was offered an internship in a well-known law firm. There, I had the opportunity to apply everything I was learning in class.

"After I finished law school, I took the bar examination and passed. The law firm where I was an intern offered me a full-time job. I couldn't believe it. So many times I went to a park near my office and sat on a bench and wondered if I was having a dream. I wasn't really a lawyer, I was just watching and imagining everything from the other side of the fence. The first and most important thing I did was to buy a house for my mother. I was able to send her enough money so she didn't have to work anymore; she could stay home. I was also able to help my brother and sister get an education. The help I received from Aunt Pedrina was so great that the whole family benefited from it.

"The rest is history. Without Aunt Pedrina's dedication and help, I could never have accomplished what I did. I am forever grateful to her. But you know, I'm not the only one in this town who owes Aunt Pedrina their education. She dedicated her life to helping people, especially underprivileged children."

When I left Airton da Silva's office, I was much more comfortable. It made me feel good to hear all those terrific things about Aunt Pedrina. She usually never talked about what she had done for other people. She used to say we should never let our left hand know what our right hand does. When I told her about what Airton told me, she became a little embarrassed and said, "I only showed him the way. He walked through all by himself." Airton and I, both beneficiaries of Aunt Pedrina's gift for teaching, became life-long friends.

Eighteen
A Special Gift

Gradually, my time with Gramma and Aunt Pedrina was getting shorter and shorter as I was becoming more involved with my education. In two more years I would be taking the examination to enroll in the national university. The preparation for the exams was difficult and demanding. I had to have the best grades I could get now in order to be accepted. I promised myself that I would get into the university on the first try, which was not easy. I continued to visit them as much as possible, but I had to cut down on the time I spent there. Even when I visited them, I spent most of the time with my books. I missed the time we spent together doing fun things, like digging in the front yard and finding gold or paddling Audacity. Audacity was the name of Aunt Pedrina's canoe. They understood my lack of time. In fact, Gramma and Aunt Pedrina were proud of me for taking seriously my responsibility toward getting a good education. I also missed the summers when Aunt Pedrina and I used to get involved in so many interesting projects.

The Christmas holidays I always spent with Aunt Maria de Lurdes and Uncle Jose. They requested we stay together this time of year as a family, which, as far as I was concerned, was the right thing to do. They raised me and were very generous in providing the best for my physical and mental development. Aunt Maria de Lurdes, like most of the women in my family, was a teacher. Since she didn't teach at any school, I was her only student. She was extraordinarily patient and an excellent tutor.

One particular holiday season, they planned to go to Portugal, where we still had lots of family. Uncle Jose thought it would be the perfect time to go visit with them, since everyone was getting old and they didn't have many opportunities to visit. They thought Christmas was the ideal time to go, but I could not take much time off because of my studies. I decided not to go to Portugal and, instead, go visit with Gramma and Aunt Pedrina, only for the holidays. I called Gramma and told her about my plans. Needless to say, she and Aunt Pedrina were pleased with my decision.

Because of my tight schedule, and also because I wanted Aunt Maria de Lurdes to help me, as she did every year, with my selection of gifts before she left for Europe, I started my Christmas shopping early. Aunt Delores, cousin Lucia, and Uncle Miguel were easy to buy for; earrings for cousin Lucia, a gold charm for Aunt Delores's bracelet (she collected those things), and for Uncle Miguel a silk tie. He would like that. Olinda and Yolanda would both get a pretty sweater. For Gramma, it was even easier. She had a beautiful dollhouse, an antique, and she liked to collect miniatures for it. Aunt Maria de Lurdes knew a place that specialized in miniature furniture and accessories for dollhouses. I bought a marvelous, miniature Tiffany-style lamp. The problem was Aunt Pedrina.

Aunt Pedrina did not collect anything that I knew of. She didn't like to wear jewelry, except for the engagement ring she hung on a gold chain and wore around her neck so she wouldn't lose it again. Clothing was totally out of the question. She liked to read, but she was a member of every book club under the sun and received by mail the latest bestsellers. She was very easy to get along with, but extremely difficult to choose a gift for.

I wanted to give her a special gift, something she would love and treasure. What could this be? A tough question, for which I had no answer. The only hint I had was that she loved plants. She always was finding plants that were rare or somehow special. She loved to show off her plants to her friends when they came to visit. I could get her a plant as a gift, but it had to be something rare or unique. I started a search for that one-of-a-kind floral species.

Time was running out. I had been in almost every single plant shop I knew of but had not come across the kind of magnificent floral extravagance I was looking for. A friend of mine, who, like everyone, knew I was shopping for an unusual plant, told me about a brand new shopping center that had just opened before the holidays. It had elegant shops and an exclusive flower and plant store. She suggested I give it a try. I decided to go see it.

It was, undeniably, a beautiful shopping center. There was a multitude of exclusive stores and a super-sophisticated flower shop full of lush, gorgeous plants. But nothing really different. I continued to look around without much hope. Almost at the end of the center, I found an exotic Oriental gift shop, with a great deal of beautiful and unusual merchandise. In a corner, close to the window, a remarkable collection of Bonsai caught my attention. Whaw! I was fascinated by the miniature trees, planted in enchanting Japanese ceramic flower pots. The trees, even though so small, appeared to be ancient. No doubt they were different and distinctive, an extravagant botanic species. I felt I had found what I was looking for. I was almost sure that no one in Mirante had ever seen anything like this. She would love it. They were expensive, but she deserved it.

I had the tree placed in a special box for the trip. Two days later, I was ready to go, so my cousin Clara took me to the bus station. I looked like Santa Claus with all my beautifully wrapped gifts. The trip only took three hours and when I arrived, Gramma and Aunt Dolores were waiting for me. It was so refreshing to see them. Aunt Pedrina didn't come so there would be more space for me and my bags in the car. She would see me when we got home, they said. I didn't give the gifts to anyone; I wanted to wait until Christmas Day. I kept everything in my room and opened the tree box so it could breathe and get a little water.

Christmas morning I was excited. Everyone was coming to Gramma's house for dinner; we were going to have a great time. Gramma, Yolanda, and Olinda were busy in the kitchen preparing the big holiday feast. After breakfast, I told Gramma I was going to Aunt Dolores's house to give her, Lucia, and Uncle Miguel their gifts, and then I would go to Aunt Pedrina's. At Aunt Dolores's house, I placed the boxes under the Christmas tree and told them I would see them later at Gramma's and I left. I couldn't wait to get to Aunt Pedrina's. I was anxious to see her reaction to my unusual gift. When I got there, I knocked on the door, knowing she would be the one to greet me since Olinda was at Gramma's. When the door opened, I was holding the box in front of me to hide my face. "Merry Christmas! Ho, ho, ho!" I said, making the kind of embarrassing imitation of Santa's voice that only close family think is cute.

"Merry Christmas to you, too, young Santa," she said, laughing. "Come in and have some cookies and milk."

I walked in, closing the door behind me. "Aunt Pedrina, you're going to love this. I'll bet this is going to be your favorite gift. I'm sure you've never seen anything like this," I was excited. I opened the box and exclaimed, "Taran! How do you like it?"

"Oh, a Bonsai," she said, much less enthusiastic than I had expected.

"You know about these miniature trees?" I asked, kind of disappointed.

"Well, I read about it a long time ago. I believe they are originally from Japan. They do with the trees the same thing they used to do with women in China," she explained somberly.

"What? What's the connection between women in China and this miniature tree?" I was completely lost.

"Today is supposed to be a happy day, a day of celebration and family reunion. You don't want to hear about that," she said, placing her arm around my shoulder.

"Oh, yes I do! I'm very interested to understand what you're talking about. I'm confused about this." Really, more than confused. Now I was intrigued by Aunt Pedrina's reaction to the Bonsai. I didn't want to miss one of her stories. This particular one had a promise of some Oriental mystery.

"First of all, this is not a miniature tree," she said pointing to the Bonsai. "This is a normal tree that has been stunted. In Japan, they developed a technique of pruning and feeding a tree in a controlled manner which will slow or stop growth. As the plant ages, it acquires this look of an old miniature tree. They developed a way to manipulate nature. Do you understand?" she asked.

"Yes, I think so. And I don't believe that's a nice thing to do," I said uneasily. "But what about that thing with women in China? It still doesn't make sense to me."

"In many parts of the world," she started, "women were not treated with respect. They were treated more like an object, a private possession rather than a human being.

A long time ago in China, in some rural villages, when a woman gave birth to a girl it was a day of sadness and disappointment. They wanted to have a boy because a son could work in the field and help the family survive. A daughter was another mouth to feed; they had no purpose. And, usually, they couldn't afford another mouth to feed. Sometimes, they threw the newborn girl into the river to drown.

"In the city, when a family didn't have political power or money, a beautiful daughter could be their only asset. They groomed and educated the girls, but their education was nothing but an extensive training in how to care for and please a man. This would make the girls more attractive to a rich man, if possible rich and powerful. The father was in charge of this exchange. He would try first to marry the daughter to a rich man who could help the family with money and special jobs. If he did not succeed, the next step he would try to sell the daughter as a concubine for a very rich man with powerful political connections, hoping they would get some of the same benefits."

"What about the daughter? Didn't she have anything to say about this?" I asked. I understood, from my studies at school, that my question was based on my Western values.

"No. Like I said, women were nothing more than objects. The father was the one who would make decisions concerning the girls' lives. When someone is going to sell or trade an item, he or she wants to have a perfect one," Aunt Pedrina continued. "Small feet were considered a most desirable mark of beauty. Men were attracted to young girls with very small feet; the ideal size was no more than three or four inches."

"Where did you learn about that? This is really strange," I said, glancing sideways to the 'miniature' tree next to me.

"By reading. Many books have been written about this cruel practice. In the West, we like to point out bad things of the East to divert our attention from the wrong things we do as well," she said seriously.

Almost afraid of hearing the answer, I asked, "What happens when the girl didn't have small feet?"

"Well, that is the similarity with the Bonsai. They developed a technique to stunt the growth of the feet. It is the most painful and cruel thing I have ever heard. The mother bound the little girl's feet when they were very young, two or three years old. They bent all of the toes, except the big toe, under the foot, pressed against the sole. They placed a stone on top of the foot and wrapped a long narrow cloth around the foot and the stone, binding them together. They wrapped the cloth so tight that when the foot grew and forced against the cloth and the stone, the foot bones broke, causing excruciating pain. The little girls would scream day and night for a long time, maybe several years. Sometimes the pain was so overwhelming, they fainted."

"My goodness," I couldn't believe it. "What happens to the feet? How could they walk after that? This is really terrible."

"The foot would remain small and permanently deformed, like a small, old foot," she said, pointing to the Bonsai. "They covered them with embroidered silk little shoes to hide the ugliness of the feet, like this beautiful porcelain flower pot. As far as walk, they couldn't do much of it. They had to be carried, or when they did walk, they did it by little jumps, almost like a bird. It was believed that men found this little walk enchanting. If the girls were pretty with small feet, chances were they would marry a rich man or be sold as a concubine to a powerful man. In either case, they would have many servants and would do nothing but please their man. There was a big market for beautiful concubines in China. A man could have only one wife, but many concubines, as many as he could afford. They used their concubines to display power and wealth."

"How could a mother do this to her own daughter?" I asked in disbelief.

"It was a difficult task. If the mother felt sorry for the little girl and unbound her feet, allowing them to grow to normal size, the girl would later blame the mother for destroying her life. With normal sized feet, they would be ridiculed and wouldn't be able to obtain a good marriage, which was the only purpose of their life. They would marry a poor man and would be a servant, which was almost the same as being a paid slave. Attaining a good marriage or being sold as a concubine was the only future for young women. They were the victims of their own culture and traditions. It was a sad situation."

"I'm sorry. I thought this was a wonderful, special gift. I had no idea the Bonsai was a constriction of natural growth. And your story about the similarity to foot-binding makes me feel sorry for the little tree. I'll take it back."

"No, no. It's not your fault, you didn't know about that. I'll keep the Bonsai," she said, holding the flowerpot.

"But, you don't like the tree for what it represents. I don't think I like it either," I said.

"I understand, but I want to keep it because you and I are going to do something wonderful," she replied, smiling slyly and giving me her naughty look. She was her old self again.

"What are we going to do?" I asked. I couldn't figure out why she would want to keep it.

"First of all, we are going to take this poor tree from this fancy pot. Then, we're going to find a good place in the backyard and plant it. I'm going to give it lots of love and care and make sure it gets plenty of sun and enough water.

In no time, we are going to have the biggest Bonsai in the Western Hemisphere. What do you think?"

"Oh, I like that. It's a great idea. Let's do it," I said eagerly.

"This is an easy problem to solve," she said. "I wish we could do the same for all of the oppressed people around the world. In many places they are treated just like this poor tree. They aren't allowed to grow, their hopes and dreams pruned and stunted. I would like to have the opportunity to go to these places and nourish them, giving them love and an opportunity to learn and grow to free-minded people, capable of helping themselves and making it possible for their dreams to become reality. That way, they could be strong, good, and happy people. I'm sorry, dear, but I think it's getting late. It's time to go to Gramma's. Let's enjoy tonight's dinner and the company of our family and friends. Let's celebrate our liberty. Tomorrow, you and I will liberate this poor tree."

It was a beautiful Christmas. We had lots of fun. Everyone liked his or her gifts, well . . . almost everyone. I received many terrific presents. I'm glad I had decided to spend that Christmas with Gramma. It was her last one. She passed away during the warm, slow month of February, before the sun moved north and the southern continent cooled through Fall. Her extended family surrounded her, standing silent and solemn, heads lowered in sadness.

Our family experienced several sorrowful losses. It was not long after we lost Gramma that Aunt Pedrina's spirit followed her.

Nineteen
The Last Farewell

I have no idea how long I had been sitting there in the corner, thinking about the stories she had told me, the lessons she had taught me, and the fun we had enjoyed together. I wish for all young people to have someone like Aunt Pedrina to help them, and love and care about them. Growing up can be a difficult and painful process, involving so many things we don't know or understand. When we have someone who has the ability to explain why things happen when they happen and help us comprehend the difference between right and wrong, life becomes more meaningful—not easy, just more meaningful. We learn how to respect ourselves, and consequently, to respect others.

I was so involved with my recollection and thoughts that I hadn't realized the room had become full of people who had come to say good-bye to her. The whole family was there and some of her old friends, former students, or people whose lives she had touched. I recognized several of her friends, like Meg and Rogerio, Airton da Silva, Juca, Jacinto, and Anita and many others. Most of them were already outside waiting for her to be taken to the church where the memorial service was to be conducted. Aunt Dolores came and sat next to me.

"How are you doing, honey? You look tired. Did you

eat anything?" I nodded silently. "I think it would be better if you stayed with us until you have to go back to the city. If we're together, it will be less painful. We'll help each other overcome our loss. She was my favorite aunt. I'll miss her forever."

"Thank you. That's nice, but I already promised Aunt Maria de Lurdes I would go back with her and Uncle Jose. I think it's better for me to go with them," I answered.

"Honey, it's time to say good-bye. They are going to close the coffin and they won't open it again. Come, I'll go with you," Aunt Dolores said, standing up.

"No. Thanks, but I don't want to say good-bye to her in that box. I've spent the whole day thinking about the wonderful things we did together, the smart and insightful words she spoke to me. I have a vivid memory of her. In my mind she is very much alive. I don't want to simplify or reduce her entire life into this brief moment of her death. I have a feeling that if I bid farewell to her that way, I will bury my memories with her body.

"She had a beautiful and meaningful life, and that's what I wish to celebrate. I want to remember her life and keep the memories of her with me forever. She'll continue to be alive in my thoughts. That way, everything she taught me will still be fresh, helping me to become the person I want to be. I don't want her death to overshadow her life. I'm going to the church," I said, getting up to leave, "and wait there for the memorial."

I sat in the church, watching as it began to fill; most everyone came in behind the coffin. It had been placed on a carryall with wheels and they pushed it forward toward the main altar. Everyone walked behind the carryall, like a procession, from the viewing room where she was, into the church. When everyone was seated, Father Julio started the mass by saying a special prayer.

After the mass was over, he made a brief speech reminding us of some of the things she had done, especially her life-long projects helping others, in particular, children. When he finished, he asked if anyone would like to come up to the front to speak. Uncle Jose and several of Aunt Pedrina's friends read eulogies. The most impressive was from Airton da Silva. He had tears in his eyes when he thanked her for making it possible for him to turn his dreams into reality. He talked about how she had helped him become what he is now. He also talked about how much she cared for people, how much love she had given, unconditionally, to so many. He finished by saying, "Today is a sad day for us, but in heaven it's a happy day because all the little angels are going to have a wonderful new friend."

Uncle Jose, Uncle Miguel, Airton, and I were pallbearers. We took the coffin from the church to the hearse. There were so many flowers, it was necessary to use a pickup truck to take them to the cemetery. I rode with Meg and Rogerio. The way to the graveyard was the same that Aunt Pedrina and I had used the night we had dinner at Meg's house. I was thinking about that evening. It was more than a learning experience; it was an evening I'll never forget. I started to think of what was said about her in the memorial service. I couldn't help but remember the three questions; "Was it true?" "Was it kind?" "Was it necessary?" And, the answer for all three was a big yes! She was, indeed, everything they said.

When we got to the cemetery, her grave had already been dug. I looked into that big hole and felt uncomfortable thinking she was going to be buried there forever. Unlike her engagement ring, she was not to be found, ever again. I convinced myself it was O.K., only her body was going to be there. My memories of her, her smile, her naughty look, her wisdom, and most importantly, her love, would be with us forever.

They placed the coffin under a canopy and arranged all the flowers around it. When everyone was ready, Father Julio said the last prayer. One by one, the members of the family placed one, single daisy on top of the coffin and started to leave. Aunt Dolores gave one to Airton and told him that Aunt Pedrina always thought about him as a member of the family.

I was the last one to place the daisy over the coffin. As I was walking away, I looked back once more. It was then that I noticed an elderly gentleman, about Aunt Pedrina's age, walking slowly toward the coffin. He was tall, slender, very dignified. He looked bewildered, as he bent over the coffin and placed, gently, a bouquet of wildflowers on top. I couldn't believe it, the mysterious wildflowers! I think he had been, all the time, a short distance away, waiting for everyone else to leave so he could approach the coffin and say good-bye to her. He acted as if he was, carefully, protecting their very own secret. I felt uneasy, like I was intruding into a special, private moment. But, I couldn't help it, this was a revelation to me.

I continued to observe that beautiful moment of solitude. Then, all of a sudden, I remembered the mischievous smile when I asked her where she had picked the wildflowers that were, so often, on the corner of her reading table. "Everywhere," she had said, "just everywhere." For the first time during the difficult day I felt tears rolling down my face; not tears of pain, but tears of joy. I was happy for her. She had fooled everyone. I guess, contrary to what everyone had thought, including me, she was not really alone.